PRAISE FOR

THE SEA TURTLE'S CURSE

A DELTA AND JAX MYSTERY

"Susan Diamond Riley's beautifully-written tale is a magical blend of fun adventure and lowcountry lore. If you love sea turtles—like me—you'll love this book! An inspiring read for all ages!"

> **—Mary Alice Monroe, *New York Times* best-selling author of the Beach House series**

"In *The Sea Turtle's Curse*, Susan Diamond Riley takes us on another great adventure with siblings Delta and Jax and their friend Darius. Set in the South Carolina Lowcountry, this mystery intrigues, entertains, and even teaches—wonderful history, geography, culture, and heroes—without being at all teach-y, not an easy thing to pull off, and she does it perfectly. Beautifully written, fast-paced with great twists, and just plain fun, this is a book that I'm eager to share with young readers!"

> **—Rebecca Bruff, award-winning author of *Trouble the Water***

"*The Sea Turtle's Curse* by Susan Diamond Riley is a beautifully written middle-grade book which follows the journey of Delta and Jax Wells, siblings who must unravel a mystery to break an ancient curse before their world is completely turned upside down. I found myself sitting on the edge of my seat, wanting to know what happens next, but not wanting the adventure to end. A remarkable tale that will make you laugh, cry, and cheer. A feel-good story that will delight readers of all ages."

> **—Dana Ridenour, award-winning author of the Lexie Montgomery series**

The Sea Turtle's Curse
A Delta & Jax Mystery

by Susan Diamond Riley

© Copyright 2020 Susan Diamond Riley

ISBN 978-1-64663-093-6

Published by

◤ köehlerbooks™

3705 Shore Drive
Virginia Beach, VA 23455
800-435-4811
www.koehlerbooks.com

To Kate—
Reading is the very
best adventure!

THE
SEA
TURTLE'S
CURSE

A Delta & Jax Mystery

SUSAN DIAMOND RILEY

Best regards,
Susan Diamond Riley

VIRGINIA BEACH
CAPE CHARLES

To my kiddos—

Being your mom (and bonus mom) continues to
be my favorite adventure.

Table of Contents

1

Watching the Boil

"It's happening!" Jax screamed.

Lit only by a sliver of shining moon over Atlantic Ocean waves, twelve-year-old Delta Wells ran to her younger brother's side.

A fiery red glow illuminated the pit of sand at the boy's feet, sand that was now churning as if alive.

A black shape emerged from the eruption, followed by another, and then another. Delta squealed and jumped back as suddenly dozens of dark creatures emerged from the spot that, just a moment ago, had been as still and smooth as any other dune on the island beach.

"Stand back," Pops called to his grandkids. "Stay out of their way!"

"Seventy-three, seventy-four, seventy-five . . . ," Tootsie counted.

Delta froze in her tracks as nearly one hundred of the creatures swarmed the sand around her, more appearing from the depths as each second passed. With movement in any direction, she would be stepping directly on the shifting mass. As they scurried toward the water's edge, Delta marveled at their speed and imagined being swept away with them into the deep ocean.

"One hundred and twenty-six," her grandmother shouted.

Tootsie had explained that only one out of one thousand baby sea turtles survived to adulthood, but she was consoled that at least her family had seen an entire nest erupt from the sand to test fate. No birds or raccoons had nabbed them as they rushed to the breaking waves, drawn instinctively by what little moonlight shone on the water. Now they would fight for their lives against sea predators that considered baby loggerhead a tasty treat.

"So, what did you think of your first turtle boil?" Pops asked.

"Awesome!" Delta said, recalling how Jax had reacted earlier that evening when Tootsie first mentioned what they were going to do.

"Gross!" he had said. "I don't want to eat boiled turtle."

"We're not doing the boiling," Tootsie had said. "The turtles in a nest make it look like the sand is boiling when they all hatch at the same time. There are several hundred loggerhead nests on Hilton Head Island, and the Turtle Team has marked those that should be about ready to hatch. Let's go find one."

Delta watched the last of the new babies, about the size of the palm of her hand, crest the breaking waves. It was hard to imagine that, if it could survive a few years, this tiny hatchling would be the size of a kitchen table.

"Jackson, stay away from there," Pops called from where he and Tootsie were standing in the surf. Pops was the only person who regularly called Delta's ten-year-old brother by his full name. Delta glanced back to see Jax leaning over the spent boil, shining his red-tinted flashlight into the remaining hole.

"They're an endangered species, and it's illegal to tamper with their nest," Pops said.

"That's right," Tootsie chimed in. "The Turtle Team will want to examine it tomorrow to make sure all the eggs hatched."

Jax stepped away from the nest and approached his sister. "Hey, Delta," he whispered. "Look what I found."

But before Delta could register that her brother had made a discovery—a discovery that would change everything—her grandmother let out a bloodcurdling scream.

"Dagnabit!" Pops shouted. "Are you okay, honey?"

In the darkness, all Delta could see was the outline of her grandparents huddled near the sand. "Jax, bring your flashlight," she said, running toward Tootsie and Pops. "What happened?"

"Oooh," Tootsie moaned as she lay sprawled on the ground. "I stepped in a hole somebody left in the sand and fell down. Ow! Careful, dear."

Jax's flashlight shone an eerie red glow on the scene as Pops leaned over his now-seated wife. Delta knew the colored cellophane over the light's lens was a Turtle Team rule. Without it, hatchlings might mistake the white light for the moon shining over the ocean and head in the wrong direction. Even so, the blood-red glow made Tootsie's accident seem even scarier.

"This is another reason people should fill in their sandcastle holes before they leave the beach," Pops said angrily. "Aside from trapping baby turtles, holes can be dangerous to people."

Jax shone his red light into the hole that had been Tootsie's literal downfall. About two feet across and nearly that deep, it sat directly next to a half-eroded sandcastle.

"Geez. The castle's not even that good."

"That's not the point, Jax," Delta said. "They didn't clean up after themselves, and now Tootsie's hurt."

Bracing herself with both arms, Tootsie sat up on the edge of the hole, her feet hidden in its darkness.

"Do you think you can stand, honey?"

"I can try."

Pops reached underneath her arms and slowly pulled upward, but Tootsie winced. "Ow! I must've twisted my ankle when I fell."

"Well, try not to put any weight on it."

Still holding his wife beneath each arm, he lifted her out of the hole.

"We'll help you walk," Delta said. "Just put one arm around my shoulder and one around Pops." As she and her grandfather helped

Tootsie hop toward the beach path, Delta shouted over her shoulder, "Fill in that hole, Jax. We don't want any more disasters."

As the kids would soon discover, though, Tootsie's fall was only the beginning.

2

Hearing the News

"Delta, you never saw what I found," Jax said, slipping into his sister's room the next morning.

"Don't you ever knock?"

"What's the big deal?" He shrugged. "You're already dressed."

Delta stood next to the daybed, tugging the comforter up. When the kids weren't visiting their grandparents for the summer, Tootsie used this room as her art studio. There were art supplies and half-completed paintings stacked everywhere. Delta had grown to like the brightness and color they brought to the room. Placing the pillows on the daybed, she glanced around and sighed. Hilton Head Island was starting to feel like home. She was going to miss it in a couple of weeks when she and Jax headed back to Chicago for the school year.

"Just look," Jax said, shoving his fist in front of Delta's face.

She slapped his hand away, but then glanced at what he held. "Wow!"

Jax cradled a white stone with five points protruding from its oval center.

"It looks like a crooked star," Delta said. "Wonder how a rock would get tumbled into that shape?"

"It's not a star. I think somebody made it on purpose."

Delta leaned closer and saw that her brother was right. There were distinct honeycomb carvings on the center. And what she had initially seen as points on a star were a head and four flippers.

"It's a sea turtle!"

"Exactly. Isn't it awesome?"

"Where'd you get it?"

"That's the weirdest part," Jax said. "Last night, after all the turtle babies hatched, I was checking the nest with my flashlight. I thought maybe one of them hadn't made it out, and I was going to help it."

"You're not supposed to do that, Jax. You're supposed to let them climb out of the nest on their own."

"Whatever," he said, rolling his eyes. "It wasn't a *real* turtle I saw. It was this carving."

Delta lifted the stone to the morning sunlight coming through the window, projecting a single dot of light onto the carpet through a small hole in the turtle's neck. She saw now that the head had carved eyes and a mouth, while the flippers were etched in a circular pattern like the textured skin of a loggerhead.

"That's weird," she said. "A carving of a baby turtle in a turtle nest."

"Well, it may be a carving of a grown-up turtle, just small. You know, like how an action figure isn't as big as a real superhero."

"Yeah, I guess," Delta said, handing the carving back to her brother. "But how do you suppose it got into the nest in the first place?"

Jax shrugged. "I've been wondering about that all night. I don't think anyone would've buried it there on purpose. Maybe it just washed ashore like a seashell a long time ago and ended up deep in the sand."

"That could be," Delta said. "But to get washed ashore, it would have had to be out in the water at some point."

"Well, I don't know. But it's mine now."

Delta shook her head. "Jax, you know it's illegal to tamper with a loggerhead nest. Even though that's not a real turtle, you shouldn't have taken it. Tootsie and Pops will flip out."

"But it's amazing!"

"Yeah, but you should put it back where you found it." Sensing her brother's disappointment, Delta put her arm around his shoulders. "I'll go with you, bud."

Jax nodded sadly as he pocketed the carving. "This was going to be my new lucky charm."

"Morning," Delta said as she entered the living room and saw her grandmother stretched out on the sofa.

"Um, Tootsie," Jax said. "Did you know you have peas on your leg?"

Delta looked over to notice that Tootsie did, in fact, have a bag of frozen peas lying across her right ankle.

"It was easier than an ice pack. I'm hoping it'll keep the swelling down."

"Still sore?" Delta asked.

Tootsie sighed. "I'm afraid so. That was quite a fall I took, so I'm trying to just be thankful I didn't break my hip."

Jax flipped on the television and plopped down on the couch right next to his grandmother's foot.

"Ow! Jax, honey, could you please sit somewhere else so my leg doesn't get jostled?"

"Sorry."

"Guys, listen," Delta interrupted. "Look at the TV."

As an alarm beeped, a bright red line flashed across the bottom of the screen: SEVERE STORM WATCH. TROPICAL STORM JACKSON HEADED TOWARD SOUTH CAROLINA COAST.

"Hey! That's me!"

"It's not funny, Jax," Delta scolded. "That storm's headed right toward us."

"Shh!" Tootsie flapped her hand in the direction of her grandkids and stared intently at the television.

"This is Judy Drench, reporting *live* from Hilton Head Island."

Despite the clear weather, the newswoman was clad in a bright pink polka-dotted raincoat and carried a matching umbrella. Delta recognized the red and white striped lighthouse in the background. She and Jax had just been to Harbour Town a couple of weeks earlier and had climbed to the top of that light.

"Don't be fooled by today's sunshine, ladies and gentlemen," Judy Drench announced, her eyes wide with excitement. "Tropical Storm Jackson is working up a lather out in the Atlantic Ocean right now and could very possibly gain hurricane strength by this time next week."

The TV reporter motioned to a nearby palmetto tree, its fringed branches barely swaying in the light breeze. "Enjoy this calm air now, because in a few days these trees will likely be bent sideways as *Hurricane* Jackson arrives on Hilton Head Island. If this storm intensifies as forecast, it could become the storm of the century."

"Wow! That sounds bad," Delta said.

"But it's still funny that it's my name," Jax laughed.

Delta groaned. "It won't be so funny if Hurricane Jackson destroys the island."

Tootsie sighed. "All we can do is prepare for the worst and hope for the best. It's just a tropical storm at this point."

Pops called from the kitchen. "Delta! Jackson! Your mom and dad want to talk to you." He popped his head around the corner of the living room door and Delta could see the telephone in his hand, the coiled cord tethering him to the kitchen wall. Tootsie and Pops still preferred to use their landline.

"Hey, Mom. Hey, Dad," Delta said as she took the receiver. "The news just said there's a big storm headed this way."

"Oh no!" Mom said. "Well, do whatever Tootsie and Pops say to stay safe."

"They've been through lots of storms on the island," Dad added, sounding as if he were speaking to them from inside a can. "They'll know what to do."

"Are you guys on speakerphone?" Jax asked, leaning into the receiver. "We don't have speakerphone here."

"Yeah, well, hold the phone so you can both hear us," Dad said, "because we have a super exciting surprise for you both."

"You'll never guess it in a million years," Mom added.

Delta perked up. Between Tootsie's hurt ankle and the approaching storm, they could sure use some good news.

"Are we finally getting a dog?"

Dad laughed. "No. No dog."

"Um, are we getting a baby brother or sister?"

"Absolutely not, Jax," Mom said. "You guys aren't even warm."

"That's a hint, by the way," Dad said, and he and Mom both burst into giggles.

Huh? What hint?

"Oh, honey, let's just *tell* them," Mom said.

"Yeah, just tell us." Delta and Jax looked at each other expectantly.

"We're moving to Siberia!" Dad shouted.

"Siberia?" Delta shook her head. "Yeah, right. What's the real surprise?"

"That *is* the real surprise, sweetie," Mom said. "You know how I've always wanted to lead a groundbreaking geology study."

Delta honestly hadn't paid much attention to her parents' professional dreams. She knew her mom worked with rocks and her dad took photos for the local newspaper, but she really hadn't given their jobs much thought beyond that.

"Well," Mom continued, "Dr. Johansen at the Field Museum had to drop out as lead geologist of a meteorite study in northern Russia, and—can you believe it?—he recommended *me* as his replacement."

"And they've offered to hire me to photograph the expedition," Dad chimed in. "We get to spend the whole year exploring inside the Arctic Circle."

"Isn't it always cold and snowy there?" Delta asked. She remembered seeing an old movie once where a Russian soldier got sent to Siberia as punishment and froze to death.

"We'll have space heaters," Dad said, "and we'll learn to dress like the locals."

Jax scowled. "Do they speak English there?"

"Most people don't," Dad replied, "but we'll have a translator working with us."

Delta's thoughts spun. *This is crazy talk.* "But, wait, how can we go to school there if we don't even speak the same language?"

"See, Delta, that's not even an issue," Mom said cheerfully. "Since we'll be traveling from place to place, we'll homeschool you wherever we are."

Delta considered that possibility. "How will you have time for that if you're both working?"

"Maybe we can do our stuff online," Jax suggested.

"Well, most places we're visiting won't have Wi-Fi," Dad said. "We're talking *real* adventure time here, guys. This is a once-in-a-lifetime opportunity!"

"We thought you'd be excited," Mom said, clearly disappointed in the reaction the big announcement had received. "Meteorites. From outer space!"

Delta and Jax stood silently, their heads together over the telephone receiver.

Dad sighed. "Just let the idea sink in a little. I'm sure it'll grow on you."

The kids said their goodbyes, and Delta replaced the phone on the wall-mounted cradle.

"I don't want to move to Suburbia," Jax said, tears welling in his eyes.

"It's *Siberia*, dumb-dumb."

"I don't want to move there, either."

Delta felt a hard lump in her throat. Her eyes stung. She turned away from her brother and dabbed a tear from beneath her lashes. "Neither do I."

3

Sensing Some Trouble

By the time Delta and Jax walked the two blocks from their grandparents' house, the sun was high and the beach was already speckled with sunbathers. A rainbow of umbrellas sprouted from the sand like blooming flowers, and scattered beach towels looked like patches on an endless blanket.

"We should have come out here earlier," Delta said. "It's already getting crowded."

A family of bikers pedaled by on the hard-packed sand, and laughter alerted the kids to the large group of wave jumpers enjoying the late morning surf. In the distance, Delta noticed several shrimp boats with their nets down, gathering the seafood that would grace the plates in island restaurants. Farther north, where the Atlantic Ocean met Port Royal Sound, she noticed a boat displaying a red flag with a white diagonal slash through it. Pops had told her that was a "diver down flag" and meant that divers were in the water below.

They must not know about Hurricane Jackson, Delta thought.

"With all these people around, it's going to be hard to bury that carving where you found it."

"It'll be hard, all right," Jax replied, "because the Turtle Team already took the stakes down, so I don't know where the nest was."

"What?"

Sure enough, the white stakes and orange caution tape that had marked last night's turtle boil were gone.

"I know it was somewhere in front of this gray house with the big second-floor deck and the half-moon shaped window. See?"

Jax pointed toward a house separated from the ocean by rolling dunes of sand and gently waving beach grass—sand and grasses that, Delta noted, all looked pretty much the same.

"Well, where do you *think* it was?"

"I don't know. It could be anywhere."

"It was by the sandcastle and that hole," Delta recalled. "The one that hurt Tootsie."

The kids twirled toward the water and eyed the surrounding area for any signs of the previous day's sand sculptures, but the smooth sand was packed hard.

"The tide came in and leveled everything out," Jax groaned. "It's all gone."

As Delta turned back toward the dunes, she noticed a commotion a few houses farther up the beach. Several people wearing bright orange T-shirts were standing in a circle looking toward the ground. About a dozen beachgoers surrounded them.

"Hey! I see some of the Turtle Team. Maybe they'll remember where that nest was."

But as they approached the team members, the kids could tell that something was amiss.

"Who would do such a thing?" one man asked.

"Do you think it was a wild animal?" another said.

Delta stepped between two adults in swimsuits and saw what had drawn everyone's attention. A nest of loggerhead eggs lay scattered on the beach in the hot sun. Three white posts and a wad of orange tape were strewn about the nest site, which was now a hole about a foot deep.

"Aw, geez," Jax said, pointing to an egg that had cracked open. "Why'd they have to do that?" Delta could see a tiny flipper poking out of the broken shell, as still as the stone carving in her brother's pocket.

"Sorry, folks, but we're going to have to ask everyone to stand back," announced a woman wearing an orange Turtle Team shirt. "Please stay away from the remaining turtle nests and remind your friends that vandalizing a loggerhead nest in *any* way is illegal in the state of South Carolina."

"I don't think we should try to bury my turtle out here," Jax whispered as he and Delta headed back toward the beach path.

"I was thinking the same thing, but we're going to get in trouble anyway if they find out you took it from a nest."

"Can we just keep it a secret then?"

"I don't think we have any choice."

Before crossing over the dunes toward home, the duo glanced back toward the ruined loggerhead nest. "Man!" Jax said angrily. "Today sucks. The only good thing to happen since last night was finding my turtle."

Delta glanced over and saw him cradling the carving in the palm of his hand. "Maybe," she replied. "But has it occurred to you that, ever since you found that turtle, everything has gone wrong?"

4

Meeting the Macs

"Been anytime interesting lately?"

Pops' question hung in the air for a moment without response as his truck traveled up the long curving drive to the Island History Museum. The kids continued their moping, staring out the window at the passing live oaks hanging over their path. Delta usually found the ancient trees majestic and soothing, their branches bending and swooping in unlikely directions like doodles scrawled in the margins of a school notebook. The Spanish moss that dangled from them had always reminded her of Christmas tree tinsel, but today the dull gray strands reminded her of dusty cobwebs in a spooky old house.

"I said, 'Been anytime interesting lately?' "

It was a favorite game between Pops and his grandkids. As a former history professor, he was naturally fascinated by the past, and no one had been surprised when he decided to head Hilton Head Island's own history museum after he retired from teaching a decade ago.

Time Machine was his way of bringing his passion to life for Delta and Jax, begun years ago when he first read them H.G. Wells' book about time travel. According to Pops, their family was distantly related to the famous science fiction author, but Delta suspected that nugget of information was just part of the game. When neither of the kids responded to today's prompt, though, Pops related his own imagined travel through time.

"I believe I forgot to tell you about my trip to the Cretaceous Period the other day. It was hot and sticky out, but I suppose you'd expect that in August."

Pausing, he glanced at Delta and Jax, who sat beside him on the bench seat of the pickup truck, still staring glumly out the window.

"So, it was just me and a herd of sauropods, minding our own business, you know. A few bolts of lightning lit up the sky, so I'm thinking maybe it's going to rain."

The crunch of tires on the oyster shell drive broke the otherwise heavy silence, so Pops continued. "Then, BOOM!"

Delta and Jax both jumped in their seats.

"Suddenly it was like bombs were falling from the sky all around us. Those long-necks took off running in a frenzy, and I had the presence of mind to jump on the back of one of them for a ride."

Jax shook his head. "You couldn't have done that, Pops. Those things were way too tall."

"Well, they were running through a sort of gully, you see, and I was on the bank above. I just jumped down on one of them as they passed."

Delta shrugged. *Maybe that technique could have worked.*

"Anyway, the bombing scared this T-Rex so bad that he ran right past us without even stopping for a nibble. We were lucky, wouldn't you say?"

The kids grunted a mild agreement. Delta sure didn't feel lucky today.

"Turns out it was a flock of pteranodons who thought it'd be funny to drop a bunch of water balloons on us as they flew over."

Despite their attempt at moping, both kids let out a chuckle. "Pops!" Delta groaned.

"Dinosaurs died out because of meteor storms," Jax added.

"You don't say?" Pops said with mock surprise. "Are you sure it wasn't water balloons, Jackson? Because that's what I saw when I was there."

"Definitely meteors."

Pops let a few seconds pass before he spoke again, this time more seriously.

"You know, your folks are likely going to find all kinds of meteorites in Siberia. That part of the world is famous for that. It really is going to be a fascinating research project and a great career opportunity for both of them."

"But what about our friends in Chicago?"

"I know you'll miss them, Delta-boo, but you've been okay without them this summer while you've been on the island with us. What's a few more months?"

Delta had to admit there was some truth to what Pops said. She'd been so busy having fun on Hilton Head that she hadn't missed her friends in Chicago like she had expected. *But Siberia?*

"It'll be so cold there. And how will we do school? I just don't know . . . I don't want to talk about it right now."

She crossed her arms and turned back toward the passenger-side window as the truck stopped. Before them stood a grand old house with a deep, shaded front porch lined with rocking chairs. Baskets of spidery ferns hung from the eaves, and crepe myrtles bloomed in shades of red, pink, and purple beside a wooden sign emblazoned *Island History Museum*. Once the home of rice planters more than one hundred fifty years ago, the once-abandoned plantation was now a favorite local site for enjoying the semitropical scenery and learning about life on the Sea Islands of South Carolina. Delta hoped hanging out here for a few hours while Pops worked would distract her and Jax from their awful morning.

Once inside, the kids gravitated toward the Lowcountry Critters room. Tanks of fish lined one wall, and a table displayed the skeleton of an armadillo and a collection of fossilized shark teeth.

"I wonder how *he* felt being taken away from *his* home?" Jax asked, admiring a baby alligator in a large terrarium.

Delta groaned. "Can we *please* not talk about that anymore?"

"You're just swimming in a river in Egypt."

She stared at her brother. "Huh? What's that supposed to mean?"

"You're in *the Nile*. Get it? Like *in denial*. You're pretending the move isn't real."

"I am not, Jax. I'm painfully aware that it's real. It's just that I don't know how to fix it, and I guess my brain is kind of on overload right now. Too many bad things seem to be happening today."

"Yeah, that *is* kind of weird."

Hearing voices coming from the museum entrance, Delta glanced out of the Critters room and saw her grandfather shaking hands with a dark-haired man sporting cowboy boots. Pops gave the man a friendly pat on the back before noticing Delta standing in the doorway.

"Delta! Jackson! Come meet some good friends of mine."

As they approached the men, Delta noticed a bespectacled boy about a head taller than her standing behind the booted visitor.

"Fellas, these are my grandkids, Delta and Jackson. They've been visiting with us from Chicago for the summer."

Delta nodded at the strangers.

"People call me Jax," her brother said.

"Well, hey, Jax. Nice to meet you!" the man replied. "I'm Daniel McGee, but people call me Mac." Jax smiled and shook Mac's hand.

"And this is my son, Darius." The boy pushed his glasses higher on the bridge of his nose as he nodded.

"The McGees are loaning their marsh tackies to the museum for display," Pops explained. "They'll be visiting regularly to tend to them."

"Nice," Delta said. "Um, what are marsh tackies?"

"They're the sweetest horses you'll ever meet," Mac said. "Isn't that right, Darius?"

The boy's dark curls bounced as he nodded. "They're the best! Spanish settlers brought them over here about five hundred years ago and left them behind. They're really rare now, though."

"That's for sure," Pops added. "There are only a few hundred alive today, but the McGees are sharing their pair with us so folks can see some true Carolina horses."

Mac turned back toward Pops. "We've got the tackies settled into the paddock by the barn, but I was hoping to pick your brain about a project I'm working on."

"Sure thing."

"You know how I've been working on behalf of the Tribal Center to put together a collection of Native American relics from the area?"

Pops nodded.

"Well," Mac continued, "the Santa Elena Center over in Beaufort has agreed to display our exhibit. We're calling it 'The First Carolinians'."

Pops gave the man another slap on the back. "That's just wonderful, Mac! Just wonderful! How can I help?"

"I've decided to present the display within a facsimile of a shell ring," Mac said, his eyes widening.

Pops grinned. "Nice!"

"What's a shell ring, Pops?"

"Just like it sounds, Jackson. A big ring made of seashells."

"To wear on your finger?"

"No, way bigger than that," Darius said. "Native American tribes around here used to build piles of discarded oyster shells all around their villages, kind of like their version of a landfill. Over time, the shells would accumulate until there was a wall of them several feet high all around the village, like a fence."

"That's right," Mac added. "That's one way we can tell today where a tribal village used to be. Even though the buildings are long gone, the mounds of shells often survive. So, we've built a miniature shell ring around the perimeter of the room we're using, and the exhibits will be displayed within that."

Pops nodded his approval.

"It's a multimedia show, with some video clips, Native American music playing in the background, plenty of posters and such. My concern, and what I was hoping you might help me figure out, is how to allow visitors to interact with some of the more sacred artifacts."

Pops scratched his chin. "That *is* tricky."

"How come?" Jax asked.

"It's important to tell our history, so folks have been really generous loaning their family treasures to us," Mac explained. "But some of the items—carvings and such—are considered holy to our people and were believed to have magical, godly powers. They must be treated with the utmost respect and should only be handled by those in the tribe who understand the relics' spiritual significance."

Jax gulped. "What would happen if the wrong person touched one of those things?" Noticing her brother's solemn tone, Delta glanced over and saw him slowly rolling something in his clenched fist. "I mean, like, would they be *cursed* or something?"

"You never can tell," Mac said, with a twinkle in his eye. "I wouldn't risk it."

The two men and Darius laughed, with Delta and Jax joining in a mere second later. But Delta knew that—just like her—Jax wasn't amused. The siblings exchanged a glance that said everything. The carved turtle tumbling in Jax's palm was not their good luck charm at all. Delta and Jax were under the turtle's curse.

5

Touching the Tackies

"Darius, would you mind showing my grandkids the tackies?"

"Sure," Darius replied with a shrug.

Pops and Mac had taken seats on the porch to continue their discussion about the First Carolinians exhibit. They sat in adjacent rocking chairs, facing the palmetto-dotted meadow that served as a broad front lawn for the museum. The tunnel of ancient live oaks curved to the left, casting moving shadows on the oyster shell drive beneath. At the end of that drive, hidden by trees and distance, lay the main road and the heavier traffic of Hilton Head's summer visitors. Right here, though, on this spot, modern commotion seemed another world away.

"Darius, do you think you'd have time to help me out with some yardwork around here this fall?" Pops added. "I know you're starting high school and all, but the young man who was working for me this summer had to head back to Charleston for the school year."

Darius glanced at his dad, and Mac nodded.

"Um, like *volunteer*?" Darius asked.

"I was thinking more of a paying job—minimum wage," Pops assured. "Maybe a few hours on Saturdays?"

Darius grinned. "Wow! That'd be great!" He paused, the smile sliding from his face. "If it's okay with my mom, I mean. I usually help out at the restaurant on Saturdays."

"I'll clear it with her," Mac said. "We've got the whole extended family to work at the Grill. I believe we can spare you on Saturdays."

Darius' smile returned, and he leaned over to shake Pops' hand. "Thanks so much, sir. I promise I'll do a good job."

Pops chuckled. "I know you will, or I wouldn't have asked in the first place. But now, go tend to those tackies."

Darius led the way down the porch steps and along a tire-rutted path that ran around the side of the old plantation house. The trio of kids passed silently through a shower of bright pink crepe myrtle blossoms floating in the warm breeze like a confetti blizzard. Delta brushed the tiny blooms from her hair as the kids approached a white wooden building about the size of a two-car garage. Although there had once been a barn—perhaps several—on this land during its rice plantation days, none was left by the time Pops opened the museum. Delta remembered when the barn had been built just a few years ago, a replica of what might once have been there.

The kids rounded the corner of the building and came upon the fenced paddock. Delta had never paid much attention to the corral, never wondered why it was there. She supposed now that Pops had been hoping all along to add some marsh tackies to the Island History Museum's list of features. Now, thanks to the McGee family, here they were.

"Hey there, Indy!" Darius called as a small, sturdy black horse whinnied and ran toward him from the other side of the paddock, its long mane flapping.

Darius reached across the fence and stroked the tacky's snout. "This is Indigo. He's six years old and loves to run. He's even won some races."

"Wow!" Jax said, reaching through the fence slats to pat Indy on the chest. "Like the Kentucky Derby?"

"Nah, marsh tacky races. Sometimes we race them on the beach over on Daufuskie Island. It's more private over there. We're not allowed to do it here on Hilton Head."

Delta imagined a crowd of sunbathing tourists scattering like startled gulls as a herd of horses suddenly came racing through the surf. A caramel-colored horse approached and snuffled its nose against her shoulder.

"What's this one's name?" she giggled.

"That's Honeybee. We call her Honey."

Delta cradled Honey's chin in one hand, running the other over the horse's warm cheek. "She's sweet like honey, that's for sure."

Indigo nuzzled at Darius' pocket, and the boy reached in and offered him a handful of sugar cubes. Sensing the treat, Honey approached for her share, too.

"They're really smart and hard workers because they're so strong. That's why the Spanish explorers brought them over here in the first place and why the tribes kept using them after that."

"You and your dad sure seem to know a lot about Native Americans," Delta said after a few moments of comfortable silence focused on the friendly horses.

Darius shrugged. "Well, sure. They're our people."

"*You're* Native American?" Jax said. "But McGee isn't an Indian name."

Delta gave her brother a wide-eyed look. *"Jax!"*

"That's okay," Darius assured. "My dad's *mother* was from the Catawba tribe, but his *father's* family was originally from Scotland."

"So you're half Native American."

"Not quite. Dad is half, but I'm one-fourth. My mama is Geechee."

"Wait. Is that a different tribe?" Delta asked.

Darius rolled his eyes and chuckled. "She's Gullah. You know, Gullah Geechee."

The siblings stared blankly at their new friend.

Darius sighed. "Okay. So the Gullahs are descended from freed slaves. My mama's ancestors were from Africa, and then they were slaves here in the Lowcountry, and now we still live here. The Gullahs have their own kind of language and food and customs and stuff. Sometimes we're called *Geechee*, after a river near Savannah. My mama's family runs a restaurant here on the island—the Geechee Grill."

Jax nodded. "Oh, so you're black?"

"*JAX!*"

Delta turned to Darius. "I am so sorry for him. He always says whatever pops into his crazy head, like the *minute* he thinks it."

"No, really, it's okay. I am African, and Native American, and European. My mama says I'm a gumbo—a stew made from a little bit of everything."

Delta thought for a moment. "Hmm, our dad's family is from England or France or something, but our Mom's family is from Cuba. So I guess we're kind of a gumbo, too."

"Just with fewer ingredients," Darius added. All three kids burst out laughing.

As the siblings helped Darius lead Indigo and Honey into their stables in the barn, Delta noticed that her brother was being unusually quiet. He didn't say a word as they checked that the horses had fresh hay and water and patted them goodbye before heading back up the path toward the museum building.

"Thanks for introducing us to Indy and Honey," Delta said as they left the paddock behind. "They're really awesome." She sighed. Meeting the horses was about the only bright spot in an otherwise awful day.

"Darius," Jax finally spoke up. "Say somebody really did get cursed by some random Native American relic. How could they break the curse?"

"I think it would depend on how they got cursed. You know, like did they steal a relic or damage it?"

"What if it was neither?" Delta said. "What if they just found it by accident and didn't know it was sacred? I mean, just hypothetically speaking."

Darius gave the situation some thought. "If the curse was because they weren't supposed to have the relic in the first place, then I guess they'd have to return it to where it really belonged."

"You mean, where they found it?" Jax asked.

"Sure, if that's where it belonged," Darius said. "It would need to be put back in its real home."

Delta pondered that point. Surely the turtle carving didn't really belong on the beach. It seemed to have just washed up there. If it was truly a tribal relic, where would its *real home* be?

"Um, on a completely different subject," Jax said, "were there any Native American villages right here on Hilton Head Island?"

Darius shrugged. "Sure. Lots of them. Records from early explorers and settlers say so anyway. And there's the shell ring, of course."

Delta and Jax shared a glance. "The shell ring?"

"Yeah, well, what's left of it. It's about five hundred years old."

Delta's heart raced. "Right here on Hilton Head?"

"Not far from here, in fact. You know where the old Gullah cemetery is up Baynard Road, by the Baptist church?"

"I think so," Delta responded.

"The shell ring's just behind that cemetery. The village was right on the banks of the marsh leading out to Port Royal Sound."

Delta knew Port Royal Sound was the large bay on the northern shore of the island—a bay that opened directly onto the Atlantic Ocean and the beach where Jax had found the carved turtle.

The kids arrived at the old plantation house and saw that the rocking chairs were sitting still and empty now.

"They must've gone back inside," Darius said, ascending the porch steps.

As their new friend entered the building to reunite with his father, Delta grabbed her brother's arm and pulled him aside. "We have to find that shell ring," she whispered. "We've got to take that turtle back home."

6

Passing by Tombs

Pops dropped his keys on a hall table as he led the way into the house. Tootsie was still stretched out on the living room sofa, her leg propped on a throw pillow.

"How're you feeling, honey?"

"I don't know, dear. I've been icing it and keeping it elevated, but it's more painful than ever."

Leaning over his wife's leg, Pops gently touched her swollen ankle, which Delta now noticed had turned the color of grape soda.

"Ow!"

"Sorry, but it feels warm to the touch, and the bruising is much worse than it was this morning."

"Do you think I broke a bone?"

"I think we should go to the emergency room and get it X-rayed. That's what I think."

"Okay," Tootsie said, attempting to rise from the sofa. "Just let me fix the kids some dinner first."

"We can make ourselves something to eat," Delta said. "There's leftover chicken from last night in the fridge. We'll have that."

Pops patted her shoulder. "That'd be great, Delta-boo. Do you mind if I go ahead and take your grandmother to the hospital? We could be stuck in the ER for hours, so I don't imagine you'd want to come along. Will you kiddos be alright here alone for a while?"

"Sure. No problem," Delta said, a grand idea coming to mind.

An evening alone was exactly what she and Jax needed.

The sun was sinking behind the trees by the time Delta and Jax pulled their bikes up to the old iron fence surrounding the Gullah graveyard. Although they had never been to the cemetery before or even to the Baptist church across the street, they had passed it lots of times on the way to Pops' favorite seafood market farther down Baynard Road.

Like fingernails on a chalkboard, the creak of the rusty gate made Delta wince as she swung it open just enough to squeeze through. She glanced around quickly to see if the noise had attracted attention, but the parking lot of the church behind them was empty and no one was in sight. On their side of the street, thick woods flanked the graveyard.

Shaded by towering trees, the cemetery was darker than the early evening hour would suggest. Light filtered through the chaotic branches of live oaks, and wind whispered through the swaying fronds of palmetto trees. Before her, Delta saw a city of miniature buildings and tombstones, some leaning precariously as if too tired to stand.

"What are those little houses?" Jax asked.

"They're crypts." Delta had once seen a horror movie about a vampire who spent his days in one of those. "It's a place to put all the caskets for a particular family."

"Like, they store empty coffins there until they need one?"

"No, Jax. They put dead-body-filled coffins in there instead of burying them."

Jax scrunched his nose. "Ugh! Why would they do that?"

"I don't know. I guess the relatives all want to spend eternity together or something." Delta pointed to the words engraved on the front of a stone crypt directly in front of them: *Never alone.* She supposed the sentiment was supposed to be reassuring.

"Geez, I'd rather be alone than stacked up with a bunch of skeletons," Jax said.

"Well, you'd be a skeleton, too, so I don't think you'd care."

Jax shrugged and moved on down the aisle of stone, stopping occasionally to read the names and dates carved into the monuments.

Delta inhaled deeply. She noticed a distinct odor—salty and earthy, like life and death combined. Looking beyond the line of trees on the far side of the old Gullah graveyard, she saw the evening sunlight dancing on the marsh waters and recognized the source of the familiar smell. It was the tang of pluff mud, that slick goo revealed by receding tides in the Lowcountry marsh. A mix of decaying sea life and saltwater grasses, the rich mud nourished the living plants and oyster beds above. The scent usually made Delta feel safe and somehow at home. Here, though, surrounded by tombstones in the dying light and standing atop who knows how many dead bodies, it just seemed creepy.

"Jax! Where'd you go?" she asked in a loud whisper.

Her brother nowhere in sight, Delta walked up the lane of monuments where she'd last seen him. Fading fake flower arrangements adorned many of the graves, with small American flags stuck into the ground near some. She stopped to examine one particularly crooked marker, its stone badly eroded. She strained to read what had once no doubt been clearly engraved: *Francis Miller. 1841-1892. Gone but not forgotten.*

Delta wondered if that was true. *Does anyone really remember Francis Miller anymore?* After all, Delta hardly knew anything about her own ancestors. Sure, she and Jax were close to Tootsie and Pops— their Dad's parents—but Mom's parents had died before Delta was born and Mom rarely talked about them. Delta sighed. How could she remember something she'd never known in the first place?

"Jax? Where are you?" she asked again as she moved on down the lane.

A cloud moved overhead, transforming the shifting shadows of the graveyard into deeper darkness as Delta heard her brother scream.

"Jax! Where are you?"

Delta twirled. "Jax?" She heard a groan.

"I'm down here."

"Down where?"

"In my grave."

"What?" Delta raced in the direction of her brother's voice. Passing a statue of an angel, its wings spread as if in flight, she rounded the side of a vine-covered crypt and pulled to a sudden stop. Before her lay a gaping, perfectly rectangular hole, about three feet wide and eight feet long—just the size to fit a coffin. Sticking out the top of the hole were Jax's waving arms.

"I'm down here in my grave."

Delta leaned over the pit, her hands on her knees. "Are you okay? What happened?"

"I was just trying to read my tombstone," Jax said, "but when I walked toward it, the tarp gave way and I fell in my grave."

"Stop saying that. Are you hurt?"

"No. The tarp kind of cushioned my fall, I guess."

Looking into the hole in the ground, Delta could see now that her brother was standing on a piece of bright blue plastic, the kind that Pops sometimes used to cover supplies in his truck bed.

"See?" Jax told her, pointing toward the monument rising from the edge of the pit. "It's *my* tombstone." Sure enough, carved into the marble marker in bold letters was the single word JACKSON. "I'm too young to die!"

"Oh, brother." Delta rolled her eyes as she brushed away a clump of Spanish moss that had fallen from a tree dangling overhead, revealing the rest of the monument. "Is your name *Harrietta* Jackson?"

"Oh." Jax laughed. "That's a relief."

Delta knelt by the grave and reached for her brother's arms. "Grab hold, and let me pull you out."

The siblings clutched each other's wrists, and Delta counted to three. Jax jumped as she tugged so that he landed on his stomach half in and half out of the pit. Dragging him onto the ground as she stepped backward, Delta released her hold and promptly landed sitting in a pile of discarded flower arrangements.

"I love you, buddy, but sometimes you drive me crazy."

Jax shrugged. "I know. I drive a lot of people crazy, but I don't let it bother me."

Delta groaned as she stood, laughing. It would be nice to have her brother's self-confidence. As she brushed rotting flower petals from the seat of her pants, a loud clap of thunder caused both kids to jump.

"Um, Delta. There's something behind you," Jax whispered.

She turned slowly as a shadowy figure stepped from behind a nearby crypt. Delta thought again of the vampire movie she had seen. Wind whistled through the palmettos as a deep voice spoke.

"What are y'all doing out here?"

7

Standing in Shells

A flash of lightning lit the cloud-shielded graveyard and revealed the face of a looming figure.

"Darius! What are you doing here?" Delta asked, sighing with relief.

"I live here. What are *you* doing here?"

"You live in a graveyard?"

"Yeah, right, Jax. I live in a graveyard." Darius laughed. "My house is right over there—*next door* to the graveyard."

Delta glanced in the direction he was pointing and saw, through the trees, a house up on stilts. A wide porch wrapped around the front and side of the house, high above the ground. She imagined the view of the marsh from up there would be amazing.

"I was fishing from our dock when I heard somebody scream . . . never thought it'd be you, though."

"We were looking for the shell ring," Delta explained.

"But then I fell in my grave," Jax added.

Delta gave him a sideways glance. "We've been over that, Jax. It wasn't your grave."

Darius looked at the tombstone and nodded. "Yeah, Mrs. Jackson's funeral is tomorrow morning. She was nearly a hundred years old."

The three kids stood silently for a moment, staring at the empty grave. Delta finally spoke.

"You said the shell ring was right behind the cemetery, but all I see behind it is the marsh."

"Well, from my house, 'behind' the cemetery is *that* way." Darius pointed to a junglelike area across the property. The area appeared thick with trees and vines.

"I don't see a shell ring there, either," Jax said.

"Come on. I'll show you." Darius led the way past rows of tombs to a small opening in the wall of jungle. "This way," he said, motioning for the siblings to follow.

"Wow! We would never have found this without you, Darius," Delta said as they wound their way along a narrow path through the dusky woods. The trio came to a sapling hanging over the path, dripping with Spanish moss, silvery in the dim light. Darius held the thin branch back as Delta passed, and the two continued.

SPLOP!

"Hey!" Jax yelled. "Watch it!"

"Sorry. I thought Delta was gonna hold the branch until you passed."

"Oops! Sorry, Jax." Delta watched her brother sputter as he swatted Spanish moss from his face. The clouds parted, lighting the path a bit and revealing patches of pure white on the dark ground. The kids hiked around a bend and arrived at a steep ivy-covered slope about as tall as Pops.

"Ta-da!" Darius said. "Welcome to the shell ring."

Delta and Jax stared blankly at the jungly rise before them.

"*This* is the shell ring?" Delta asked.

"It doesn't look like seashells *or* a ring," Jax added.

"This is just one part of it. It'll look more like a ring once we're on the inside."

Delta shrugged and began scaling the slope, using vines to pull herself up through the foliage. Palmetto shrubs scratched at her arms as she huffed to reach the top of the wall that once surrounded the Native American village.

"Whew! I made it," she said triumphantly, only to see Darius and Jax staring up at her from inside the ring. "How'd you guys get down there so fast?"

Jax pointed at a spot to her left. "There's an opening in the ring right over there. We just walked through."

Delta groaned and half-slid down the inner slope into the shell ring, grabbing plants to slow her descent. Once inside, she observed a flat area about the size of a football field, surrounded by the steep plant-covered slope. Although less wooded than the jungle they had just passed through, the interior of the ring was still home to plenty of trees and shrubs, with spots of clearer ground.

"How did a whole village fit in here with all these trees?"

"Most of these trees weren't here then," Darius explained. "Remember, we're talking hundreds of years ago."

"I don't even see any shells," Jax said.

"Oh, they're here. You just have to look for them." Darius led the siblings over to a section of the slope covered with fallen leaves. Brushing the natural rubbish aside, he revealed sandy black soil beneath, speckled with flecks of white. Delta realized now that the pure white spots they had seen along the pathway just outside of the ring were the same as these—oyster shells. "Let me show you a place where you can see them even better."

Delta and Jax followed Darius along the perimeter of the shell ring until they arrived at a spot where a subtle path had been flattened in the covering foliage. Climbing to the top of the wall, the kids had a clear view out over the marsh that led toward Port Royal Sound. They stood in awe at the rainbow scene before them, the sky glowing in shades of pink and purple as the bright orange sun began to sink beneath the horizon. Below it, marsh grasses adorning the myriad oyster beds swayed in the breeze as the brilliant colors of the sunset reflected on the salty seawater. A snowy egret took flight in search of its nightly roost as a lone canoer laughed while paddling toward the Sound. The kids watched the light reflect off the long black hair of the girl as her canoe glided behind an islet of grasses and out of sight.

"Anyway, here's what I wanted to show you," Darius said, breaking their reverie. He pointed down toward an outer section of wall that had partially collapsed toward the marsh, exposing mounds of tightly packed oyster shells that composed the interior of the structure.

"Boy! They must have really loved oysters."

Darius laughed. "I guess they did, Jax, but mainly because oysters were just so plentiful around here. They never had to worry about starving, that's for sure."

As the trio slid back down the embankment, Darius spoke again. "That's cool, Jax. What is it?"

Delta looked at her brother and realized, to her horror, that he was absently rolling the carved turtle in his palm again.

"I found it in a turtle nest," he replied. "I think it's cursed."

"JAX!" Delta snatched the carving from her brother's hand and turned to Darius. "We know you're not supposed to bother a loggerhead nest, but when we tried to put the carving back, we couldn't find the nest anymore."

Darius inspected the relic cradled in Delta's hand. "It looks like a Native American piece. But why do you think it's cursed?"

"Because *everything* has gone wrong since I found it," Jax admitted.

"That's right." Delta nodded. "Our grandmother fell and hurt her ankle, and then someone totally destroyed a turtle nest on the beach. Then we heard a hurricane is coming . . ."

"It's still a tropical storm right now," Darius said.

"Yeah, but it *could* become a hurricane," Jax said.

"The very worst thing is that our parents called and said we're moving to Siberia!" Delta added.

Darius stared at her, his mouth agape. "For real? Like, in Russia?"

Delta nodded.

"And I fell in my grave." Jax looked between Darius and Delta. "Mrs. Jackson's grave, I mean."

Darius shook his head slowly. "Wow. Y'all really are having a string of bad luck. So I guess that's why you were asking me earlier how somebody could break a curse."

The siblings nodded. Delta had to admit it felt good to share their worries with someone else, especially someone who might know how to help.

"We thought if this was a real Native American relic, maybe it belonged here—you know, in a real tribal village. Maybe its original owner lived here."

"Hmm. Maybe. Where'd you say you found it?"

"It was in a turtle nest that hatched on the beach last night," Jax said.

Darius held his chin in his hand, deep in thought. "The beach facing the Atlantic or the beach facing Port Royal Sound?"

"Kind of on the corner of both," Delta said. "We were up near the tip of the island that faces both ways, where the Sound meets the ocean."

"We figured it probably washed ashore sometime and has just been buried in the sand," Jax added.

Darius nodded. "I guess that makes sense. So you were just going to leave it here?"

"Yeah, unless you have a better idea," Delta said. "We hadn't really thought it through any further than finding the shell ring."

"No, I think this is probably a good spot, although I wouldn't just leave it out in the open. People wander through here sometimes, and if the carving really is cursed, you don't want to pass that on to somebody else. I think we should bury it."

Delta smiled. Maybe she and Jax weren't completely unlucky after all. They had found a new friend who believed in them and was willing to join their crazy task.

"Where exactly should we bury it then?"

As the boys scouted out the space, Delta wandered to the very center of the shell ring. Spinning slowly in a circle, she saw that the now-vine-covered barrier was an equal distance from her in every direction. She figured that, from here, she could survey the entire area and determine a likely spot to dispose of their cursed turtle. She held it up and examined the smooth, cool stone. The white turtle shone pink in the watercolor light of the sunset, and she let her finger gently trace the intricate honeycomb carving on the animal's back.

Everything happened so gradually that she didn't notice at first that the turtle was becoming warmer or that the pink cast had become a rosy glow. She didn't even notice that fog had rolled in and surrounded her feet. In fact, Delta didn't notice these changes at all until the mysterious fog had entirely engulfed her. She stood in the haze still clutching the now-blazing red turtle.

8

Joining the Tribe

The fog surrounding Delta faded as suddenly as it had appeared. Sunset had immediately turned to midday, leaving her squinting into the brightness and sticky heat of an August afternoon. Across the way, she could see the wall of oyster shells where, just moments ago, she had been standing with Jax and Darius, staring out over the salt marsh that led out to Port Royal Sound and the ocean beyond. Those waters were likely the same as before. Everything else, though, had changed completely.

Gone were the myriad live oaks, palmettos, and pine trees that had filled the space within the shell ring. In their place, the now-cleared field was host to a circle of nearly twenty round shelters, their walls thatched with dried sea grasses and their roofs shingled with layers of palmetto fronds. Some buildings, she noticed, had no walls at all. Rather, they were open to the soft breeze blowing through the village, their roofs providing shade from the hot summer sun.

Even the shell ring itself was different, Delta now realized. Where she had just seen vines and leaves covering the wall of oyster debris, now the barrier was snow white, the seashells appearing fresh and new. Time had not yet taken its toll on this site.

"Jax! Darius!" Delta spun to find her companions, but they were not to be seen. Instead, she was in the company of dozens of the village's inhabitants, busy with their daily tasks and apparently oblivious to the odd girl in their midst.

Nearby, dark-haired women and girls garbed in animal-skin tunics bustled within one of the open-walled shelters. Branches had been lashed between two of the support posts, creating a worktable where the group appeared to be preparing some sort of meal. Delta could hear them laugh and chat as they worked, although their words were foreign to her. An open fire crackled in a sandy area in front of the shelter, where a gray-haired woman stirred a clay pot of bubbling liquid.

Delta jumped as two tattooed men in loincloths nearly walked into her but passed by as if she were invisible. One held an armload of netting, which the other helped him stretch between two wooden posts stuck into the ground. A boy about Jax's age ran toward them then, carrying the string of fish likely caught in that very net.

Hearing laughter behind her, Delta spun to see several men surrounding a cypress log, fire shooting from its center. She watched as they used large, curved oyster shells to scrape the ash from the burning wood, gradually hollowing its center to transform it into a canoe.

All work stopped, though, when a woman in a woven cape strode regally through the village. Long feathers protruded from the twist of hair high on her head, and beads of stone and shells hung down the front of her intricately stitched tunic. The tribe members turned toward her and bowed their heads as she passed, trailed by three nearly identical teenage girls. The quartet marched directly toward Delta, who froze as they stopped just steps before her.

Without so much as a glance in Delta's direction, the woman began to speak loudly in a long-forgotten language. Residents from throughout the village had gathered to hear, nodding periodically in agreement. When the woman raised her arm and pointed, all heads turned.

Delta followed their gaze and realized that what she had first taken as an old tree trunk standing in the center of the village was actually a carved statue. She had learned about totem poles at school, but this one didn't have a stack of faces. Instead it portrayed a life-sized loggerhead sea turtle.

The woman spoke again, and all attention returned to her as she lifted her arm. Three strands of beads dangled from her hand, each with an amulet of some sort hanging from it. The three girls stood solemnly as the woman draped a strand around each of their necks.

Once all three girls were adorned, they looked toward the gathered crowd and smiled shyly. Straining to see the amulets, Delta was startled when the entire village began whooping and cheering. What had she just witnessed?

As the crowd began to disperse, Delta realized she was not the only non-native in the village. A young man in knee-length pants and a laced-up shirt, wearing black leather shoes and high stockings, stood quietly leaning against a support post of an open-aired shelter. His reddish hair and freckled skin contrasted with the bronze Native Americans, one of whom patted his shoulder amiably as he passed by. Delta watched as one of the trio of female teens approached the young man. They both smiled broadly as she proudly showed him her new necklace and the amulet it held—a pure white turtle with a honeycomb pattern etched atop its back.

"Hello! Earth to Delta!" Jax called.

The mystical fog had once again engulfed her and then quickly receded as Delta found herself back in the twilit ruins of the ancient village. No more shelters. No more Native Americans. Just a now-wooded field surrounded by vine-covered walls of oyster shells. It struck her that, after seeing the vitality of the village in its prime, this current state seemed as dead as the cemetery next door.

"Hey, are you okay?" Darius asked.

"Yeah, you've been standing there like a zombie," Jax added. "Didn't you hear us calling? We asked where you think we should bury the turtle."

Overwhelmed with what she had just experienced, Delta wasn't prepared to tell the boys—not just yet anyway—about this magical spot.

"I have a gut feeling we should bury it right here," she told them, stomping her foot. "Trust me."

Delta cleared the area of leaves and pine needles as Jax scavenged a large oyster shell from the edge of the ring. After digging a few inches into the soft, sandy soil, he reached out his hand. Delta handed him the carving, which he gently placed in the hole.

"So long, turtle," he said as he buried it. "Hope you like being back home."

Darius took a fallen palmetto frond and placed it atop the carving's grave. "So animals don't dig it up or something," he said with a shrug.

The three kids headed solemnly back through the opening in the shell ring, down the dark twisting path through the jungly woods, and past the rows of tombstones in the old Gullah graveyard. Darius walked with them to where their bikes leaned against the old iron fence.

"It's getting pretty dark. Y'all be careful riding home."

"We'll be fine," Jax said. "Now that we've returned the turtle, our bad luck is over for good."

Delta smiled and nodded. She knew that the carving had called this village home. *I was there and so was the turtle amulet,* she thought.

As she pedaled toward her grandparents' home in the dark, though, Delta began to wonder if there had been a fault in her logic. *Just because the turtle was inside that ancient shell ring once doesn't necessarily mean that's where it belongs now.*

She feared its curse was far from broken.

9

Getting Even Worse

The jangle of the wall phone in the kitchen roused Delta from her dreams the next morning. She stretched her arms and rubbed sleep from her eyes as Pops called from the hallway.

"Jackson! Delta! Your mom's on the phone."

"I bet she'll say that whole Siberia thing was just a joke," Jax whispered to his sister as the siblings headed up the hall.

Delta smiled and nodded. If the turtle's curse was in fact broken, no telling what great news awaited them this morning!

"Hey, sweeties!"

Once again, Delta held the phone while both kids leaned over the earpiece of the receiver.

"Hi, Mom. What's up?"

"I was just wondering if you'd given any more thought to our conversation yesterday. About our big adventure?"

"What about it?" Jax asked.

"Well, have you warmed up a bit to the idea?"

Delta laughed. *Warm up* to living inside the Arctic Circle?

"We have some details of the move that might get you more excited," Mom said. "We found out that, since we'll be traveling from place to place a lot, we get to live in a portable yurt."

"A what?"

"A yurt. It's like a round tent made of animal hides. The locals there live in them sometimes, so we'll be really authentic."

A scene of round palm-thatched shelters in an island shell ring filled Delta's mind. "We're going to be living in a tent for a year?" she asked.

"That's right. Jax, remember how much fun you had staying in a tent at Boy Scout camp?"

"Yeah, for a week."

"Well, it'll be like that, but even better," Mom said.

"Can I at least be in Boy Scouts there?"

"Sorry, buddy. I don't think they have Scouts there. Anyway, we'll be on the move most of the time, so—"

Delta glanced at her brother's frown.

"Yurts are popular now all over the world, you know," Mom said. "They're a big thing these days, with *glamping* being all the rage."

"*Glamping?*" Delta asked.

"*Glamorous camping.* All the celebrities are doing it." Mom paused for a reaction from the kids, but all she got was silence.

"Okay, so the plan is that Dad and I will pack for all of us while you two finish up your visit with Tootsie and Pops. Then we'll come down to Hilton Head in a couple of weeks to get your shots updated, and we can all fly out of the Atlanta airport together."

"*Shots?*"

"Just a few vaccines, Jax, so we don't catch any of their illnesses over there. Dad and I have already gotten ours, and it's no big deal."

"Wait. What about our house?" Delta asked.

"It'll be waiting for us when we get back. The Sandersons next door will be keeping an eye on it."

It sounded like Mom and Dad had thought of everything. Siberia hadn't been a joke after all. *This move is really going to happen,* Delta lamented.

"I've got to head to work now, but you kiddos be good and have fun. Oh, and help Tootsie and Pops get ready for the storm."

Storm? Is that still a thing, too?

Delta returned the phone to its wall cradle and headed into the living room. Pops sat in his favorite chair, dabbing a paper napkin in the pages of a book lying on the end table.

"Dagnabit! I spilled nearly my whole cup of coffee, and this is a library book, too."

The siblings exchanged wary glances before turning their attention to the morning news blaring from the television for updates on Tropical Storm Jackson. Newscaster Judy Drench was wearing a lime green raincoat dotted with palm trees. A matching vinyl hat was perched precariously atop her stiffly sprayed hairstyle. Just like yesterday, the bright sun shone down upon the scene.

"She must be burning up in that coat," Jax said.

"Just as I had predicted, ladies and gentlemen, the tropical storm is picking up speed out there over the Atlantic," the TV reporter said, standing on a beach, the sun shining. "It's calm now, but I fully expect us to experience Hurricane Jackson right here on Hilton Head by the end of the week." Judy Drench adjusted her tipping hat with one manicured hand and grinned widely into the camera, her perfect teeth glinting in the sunlight. "However, I must report that the hurricane headed our way isn't the only tragedy to hit this seemingly peaceful island."

The camera angle widened to reveal the larger scene. Behind Judy Drench, the sparkling waters of Port Royal Sound rolled gently, a single boat bobbing on the waves with its red dive flag flapping in the breeze. The reporter motioned toward the ground and the camera followed, revealing the subject of her story.

"As you can see, ladies and gentlemen, I am standing beside a desecrated lobster-head turtle nest."

A voice off camera whispered something, and the reporter cleared her throat and continued.

"*Loggerhead* turtle nest, the second to be vandalized on the island this week. These threatened animals return to Hilton Head to lay their eggs every year."

Another off-camera whisper.

"Excuse me . . . every *two to four* years, laying one hundred or more eggs in each nest."

The camera panned to the sand again, giving Judy Drench time to check her notes. She nodded and stared back toward her television audience.

"Very few of the hatchlings survive under the best of circumstances. Here, however, ladies and gentlemen, we have the *worst* of circumstances."

A close-up shot showed the ravaged nest. Just like the site Delta and Jax had witnessed yesterday, this once-nurturing spot was destroyed. Eggs, some broken, lay scattered about, with sand thrown in piles around the now-empty pit. The posts and orange caution tape that had once marked the nest as a protected area had been ripped from the ground and tossed aside in a tangle.

"Since these are an endangered species, tampering with a . . . *loggerhead* turtle nest is illegal and punishable by fine and even jail time," the reporter continued, her eyes wide. "Stay tuned to me, Judy Drench, on Channel 1 Eyewitness News for all the latest *Nest Vandal* updates."

"Who would keep doing that?" Delta asked as the television aired a breakfast cereal commercial. "Do you think it was an animal?"

"I doubt it," Pops said. "An animal would have eaten the eggs and wouldn't have bothered to remove the posts. It would have just knocked them over a bit."

Delta felt like a rock sat in the pit of her stomach. "That's just awful! Why would anyone *want* to destroy baby turtles?"

Pops shook his head and sighed.

"You got me there, Delta-boo. There's just no figuring some people."

"Oh no! Did I hear another turtle nest was vandalized?"

Delta turned and gasped. Her grandmother was hobbling up the hallway into the living room. She leaned heavily on a pair of wooden crutches, her lower right leg encased in an oversized black boot.

"What the heck, Tootsie!" Jax said.

"You kiddos were asleep last night when we got home from the ER. Turns out your grandmother has a pretty bad sprained ankle."

Tootsie nodded with a sigh.

"What's that on your foot?" Delta asked.

"A cast boot. It's attached with Velcro, so it's not as permanent as a regular cast would be."

"But hey! At least her ankle's not broken," Pops said.

Delta nodded halfheartedly. "Um, we should go get dressed."

She shot her brother a wide-eyed look and headed down the hallway, Jax following. When they were out of earshot of their grandparents, she grabbed him by the arm and yanked him into her bedroom.

"I had hoped burying the turtle would end all of this bad stuff, Jax."

"I know. The curse seems stronger than ever."

"Do you think we buried it in the wrong place?"

Last night, after her strange experience in the shell ring, Delta had wanted to believe that the turtle was sending her a sign. After a good night's sleep, though, she wondered if maybe the tribal village vision had just been a dream. The more she thought about it, in fact, the crazier her hallucination seemed. Perhaps she hadn't really been in that bustling village at all, in which case the carving probably didn't belong there, either.

"I think we need to talk to Darius," Jax said. "He'll know what to do."

10

Hanging with Ruby

Darius grinned as Delta and Jax pulled their bikes to a stop in his front yard, where he was tossing a red playground ball to a preschool-aged girl with bouncing pigtails. His house towered a full story above them on concrete stilts, a protection from occasional tidal floods.

"Hey! Long time no see."

"Who're they, Uncle D.?"

"These are my friends, Delta and Jax."

The little girl giggled as Darius hoisted her onto his shoulders.

"You're somebody's uncle?" Jax asked.

"Yeah, this is Keisha. My brother and his wife live right over there." Darius motioned toward a white cottage with blue shutters just across the yard. A larger gray home lay just beyond it.

"That's my aunt Louisa's house."

"Wow! You must have a really close family," Delta said.

Darius shrugged. "I guess so. I mean, this property has been in my mama's family for over a hundred years. Everybody sort of shares it. That's just the Gullah way."

"Y'all ready for lunch?" a voice shouted.

Delta looked up to see a woman with dark curls standing on the raised porch of Darius' house.

"Oh, I didn't know we had company," she said, waving to the visitors.

"This is Delta and Jax Wells, Mama. I told you about them."

"That's right. Did y'all know your grandparents are two of my very favorite people on this island?"

Delta giggled. "Ours, too."

"Well, are y'all hungry?" Darius' mother asked. "I've got enough food in here to feed an army. I'm trying out some new recipes for the Grill, so come on up here and tell me what you think."

They headed up the steep steps and into the house, where Delta inhaled the tantalizing aroma of fried food. Darius led the way into the kitchen and lowered his niece onto the floor. "*Mmm!* This smells great, Mama," he said, leaning over a platter of golden-brown chicken.

"That's just my regular old chicken," his mother replied, "but I'm trying something new with the mac and cheese. I put a bit of crumbled bacon in it."

"Thank you so much for lunch, Mrs. McGee," Delta said as the woman handed her a plate piled high with chicken, macaroni and cheese, deviled eggs, and a green leafy vegetable.

"You're most welcome, sweetie, and please call me Miss Ruby. Most everybody does."

"Thanks, Miss Ruby," Jax said, taking his plate and joining the others at the kitchen table. "What's this green stuff?" he whispered to Delta, although Keisha overheard and answered.

"Don't you know what collards are, silly?"

"We've seen them before, but I've never tasted them."

"Grandma Ruby makes the *best* collards." Delta watched as the little girl stuffed a forkful of the greens into her mouth, humming happily as she chewed. Delta speared a single leaf and tentatively took a bite.

"*Hmm.* These *are* good. Jax, try them."

After eating nearly everything on their plates, all four kids agreed that, while the collards were delicious, the new mac-and-cheese recipe was the highlight of the meal.

Miss Ruby smiled at the praise. "If you culinary experts say so, then I'll add it to the menu at the Grill next week and see what the customers think."

"Can we help with the dishes, Miss Ruby?"

"Thank you for offering, Delta, but Keisha's my helper today. Why don't you bigger kids go make the most of what's left of your summer."

Delta's heart fell. This happy place, with its mouthwatering food and cheerful inhabitants, had made her forget for a while that summer was indeed coming to an end. In two weeks, she and Jax would be heading to Siberia and life as she knew it would be a thing of the past. *Of course, a lot could happen between now and then,* she thought. Hurricane Jackson could ravage the island. More disasters could befall Tootsie and Pops. The Nest Vandal could destroy yet another loggerhead nest. She tried to push away bad thoughts.

"Darius, we need to talk to you about something—*alone,*" she whispered.

"Sure, let's go outside." Darius headed out the kitchen door onto a screened porch that covered the entire back of the house.

"Whoa! Look at that view." Delta froze in her tracks and absorbed the sight before her. Midday sunlight danced upon the bobbing waves of the marsh, framed by the occasional swaying palmetto tree. A long wooden dock stretched far out over the grasses, reaching like an arm for deeper waters. From this elevated height, she could see the mazelike path of the saltwater as it led between seagrass-covered oyster beds and on out to Port Royal Sound. A great white egret stood at the edge of the yard, sharing her view.

"Wow! If this were my house, I'd just stand here all day looking at the scenery."

Darius shrugged. "It is pretty, but I guess I'm just kind of used to it."

"Hey, Delta! Hey, Jax! What brings you to our neck of the island?"

They turned to see Mac sitting at a long picnic table on the porch, scattered papers covering the surface before him.

"We just had lunch, Dad. You'd better hurry or Mama'll have it all put away."

Mac jumped up, laughing as he headed into the house. "I asked her not to interrupt me while I worked on the museum exhibit, but I figured she understood *food* is always an exception to that rule."

Delta wandered over to the picnic table and glanced at what it held. Some papers were simply lists of data. Some were photos of specific artifacts, like pottery crocks, beaded clothing, and tools. Others were drawings of village scenes, buildings, and native people. She picked up a sketch showing a fishing net strung between two posts—*just like I saw last night.* Another showed a cluster of round buildings, with seagrass walls and palmetto frond roofs. *Maybe my dream was real. How could I have known that?*

"Who do you suppose drew these pictures?" she asked.

"My dad says early explorers and settlers kept really thorough records of what they saw and experienced around here. I'd say that's who made those drawings, to show what life was like in the New World."

"No way!" Jax said, grabbing a sheet of paper for a closer look.

"Careful!" Darius whispered. "That's my dad's work."

"Sorry, but look." Jax held his discovery out for them to see, and Delta gasped. The pen and ink drawing depicted a regal woman in a woven cape and intricately stitched tunic, long feathers protruding from her hair. Beside her stood three nearly identical teenage girls, each wearing a string of beads around her neck. Delta read the type beneath the drawing, describing the scene above.

"*Yupaha, Cacique* (chief) of the Orista tribe, with her three daughters, 1572."

"Nice!" Darius said. "Their chief was a woman."

"But look at that." Jax jabbed his finger at the image of the amulet hanging from each maiden's necklace.

"A turtle," Darius whispered in awe. "Kind of like the one you found, Jax."

"*Exactly* like it," Delta corrected.

She knew now that she had truly *been* there—five hundred years ago. Somehow the turtle amulet had magically transported her through time, and anything with that much power couldn't just be left buried in the sandy soil of the shell ring, its curse continuing to grow stronger with each day.

"Guys, we have to dig up that turtle."

11

Chugging toward Chugeeta

"I have to tell you guys something when we're alone," Delta whispered. "Something happened to me last night in the shell ring."

"Okay, follow me," Darius said to his friends as Mac strode back onto the screened porch balancing a plate piled with fried chicken in one hand and a glass of sweet tea in the other. "See ya, Dad. We're going outside."

Darius motioned for the others to follow him, and the trio hurried down the steep back steps to a yard filled with pink and red flowering bougainvillea bushes.

"Over here."

He led the way past a curving live oak tree from whose one nearly horizontal branch a tire swing swayed in the afternoon breeze as if ridden by some unseen spirit. Beyond the tree, Delta saw a ring of wooden Adirondack chairs circling a stone-walled fire pit. The kids plopped into the chairs, and Delta leaned forward to tell her tale.

"I should have told you guys about this last night, but I figured you'd think I was making it up, or crazy, or something. Then, this morning I decided I must have just dreamed the whole thing. But then I saw that drawing, and I knew it must have all been real."

"Hey, Darius! You want to toss the football with us?"

Delta looked up to see two teenage boys approaching the fire pit.

"Naw, I've got friends over," Darius said and then turned to Delta and Jax. "These are my cousins, Micah and C.J."

"Hey," Delta and Jax said simultaneously.

"Y'all can play, too, if you want," one of the teens offered.

Delta looked anxiously at Darius. They needed to talk, not play football.

"No, thanks," he told his cousins. "We're just hanging out for now. Maybe later."

The boys shrugged and began passing the ball back and forth within earshot of the three kids seated by the fire pit.

"Hey, um, why don't we check out the cemetery?" Jax suggested.

Delta, Jax, and Darius stood and headed toward the old Gullah graveyard that abutted Darius' yard. "Surely we can get some privacy there," Delta whispered with a laugh.

Before the trio had even reached the iron fence, though, a small voice cried out.

"Uncle D., can I play with y'all? Grandma Ruby says I helped enough in the kitchen."

Delta turned to see Keisha running toward them, her pigtails flapping.

"Are you kidding me?" Jax whispered, rolling his eyes. "There's family coming out of the woodwork around here."

Darius laughed. "Yeah, it's pretty much like this all the time. But I have an idea."

After convincing Keisha to go play football with the older boys, he switched direction and led Delta and Jax out onto the long wooden dock stretching out over the marsh. Where the dock ended, beyond the flooded field of marsh grasses, a small metal boat bobbed in the deeper water. Darius hopped down into the flat-bottomed johnboat and called to his friends.

"C'mon in. I know the perfect place to talk in private. I bet you've never heard of Chugeeta Island."

After trying in vain to shout at each other over the roar of the boat's outboard motor, the kids decided to postpone their conversation until they reached land. Delta surveyed the scene around them as they skimmed the warm waters leading out to Port Royal Sound. A blue and green world surrounded them—aqua sky, teal water, kelly-and-lime sea grasses. Only the white sandbars and black and gray living oysters broke the pattern.

"Hey, look!" Jax shouted, pointing at a dolphin following beside them. The animal raised its snout, squeaking and whistling, which sounded like laughter to Delta. Then it dove beneath the salty waters, waving goodbye with a splash of its tail.

"There she is—Chugeeta Island," Darius yelled over the noise of the motor. The little boat had not yet reached the wide-open waters of the Sound as they approached a tiny islet covered in trees. Darius maneuvered the boat up into the shallow surf, cutting off the engine and jumping overboard into water only up to his knees. Delta and Jax followed, splashing ashore and helping pull the johnboat fully onto the sandy beach. Once they had tossed their lifejackets aside and settled the boat, Darius spread his arms wide.

"Welcome to Chugeeta."

"Why's it called that?"

Darius shrugged. "Beats me. My grandpa said it's always been called that. Nobody knows why. Maybe it was somebody's name or something."

Darius led Delta and Jax up the slope of the beach and toward a dense jungle of palms. As they reached the tree line, though, Delta noticed a narrow path through the foliage. Much like their trek down the path to the shell ring the previous evening, the three kids followed this curving trail until they reached a clearing in the undergrowth.

"Whoa! This is awesome," Jax said.

Like the shell ring, this area was nearly the size of a football field.

The ground beneath them was void of plants, instead cushioned with a thick layer of fallen leaves. Dappled light speckled the soft carpet, casting a sense of timelessness on the scene. It was hard to tell if it was day or night in this glade.

In the center of the clearing stood the source of the shadowy aura—a massive live oak whose seemingly endless branches formed a canopy over the core of the islet. The main trunk of the tree was as big around as a backyard trampoline, and many of its branches were thicker than the trunks of Pops' largest pine trees. Delta stared in awe at the roller-coaster arches and dips, noting that some branches nearly entered the ground, only to rise again and continue their journey.

"I come here camping sometimes with my cousins. As far as I know, we're about the only ones that visit Chugeeta."

Delta breathed in the earthy smell of fallen leaves. "It really is amazing, Darius."

He smiled and nodded, admiring the ancient tree. "It feels kind of magical to me here, you know? Like everything else is a million miles away."

"Hey! Look at me!" Jax had climbed atop a low branch and was hiking up its slope as if it were a steep mountain trail. Once he had reached a spot well over the other kids' heads, he spread his arms wide and shouted, "I'm the king of the world!"

Delta and Darius both laughed at Jax's proclamation, but their laughter quickly turned to gasps. As if in slow motion, Delta watched helplessly as her little brother's foot slipped and he tumbled head over heels toward the ground below.

"Oof!"

Jax landed with a thump on the ground beneath the towering tree.

"Are you okay?" Delta ran to her brother, who sat up and brushed leaves from his hair and clothes.

"Yeah, I'm alright. The ground's kind of cushiony. I guess I should've known better, with the curse and all."

"I thought the curse was broken now," Darius said. "Isn't that why we buried the turtle carving?"

"That's part of what we've been trying to talk to you about," Delta said. "Everything was just as bad when we got up this morning. Maybe even worse."

"Yeah. I don't think the turtle belongs in the shell ring after all," Jax added.

"But you seemed so certain last night," Darius said. "Especially you, Delta."

"I know. That's the other thing I wanted to tell you. Both of you." She looked from Darius to Jax and back again. "Can we just sit down and talk?"

She started to lower herself to the leafy carpet, but Darius stopped her.

"Fire ants," he warned. "I know a better place to sit."

Delta watched as his foot found familiar toeholds in the main trunk of the live oak. Before she knew it, Darius was looking down at her from a ten-foot-high perch created where the tree's secondary branches diverted to follow their own individual routes.

"C'mon up. It's plenty big enough for all three of us."

The siblings carefully climbed the massive trunk, with Darius providing instruction from above. Once atop the fork, Delta saw that the crotch of the tree was covered in ferns, growing as if on the ground.

"It's like a nest up here," Jax said, laughing.

"I know, right?"

Delta sat gently in the soft ferns and gazed around her, this new perspective emphasizing the grandeur of the live oak. Even though they were ten feet in the air, she could see that the fern-dripping branches extended up beyond them. Even more amazing to her, though, was that from here, at the very core of the magnificent plant, its oaken arms stretched out in every direction, traveling farther than she could see. She was sitting at the center of *everything*.

"So, what's your big secret?" Darius asked.

The boys stared at Delta and, for the first time this afternoon, she felt she had their undivided attention. They remained quiet as she told them how the turtle carving had turned hot in her hand and how the mystical fog had rolled in and then dissipated. They sat mesmerized as she described the bustling Native American village, with its cheerful and hardworking inhabitants, the regal woman, and the three identical teenage girls.

"No way. How could you have known that?" Jax said.

"Exactly. That's why I was so freaked out when I saw that drawing at Darius' house."

"Is this for real?" Darius asked seriously. "You're not just telling a cool story?"

"No! I swear! Too much is at stake here, with Tootsie getting hurt and the hurricane coming. I wouldn't just make this up."

Jax nodded slowly and then turned to Darius. "She wouldn't. She's a pretty no-nonsense kind of girl."

The trio sat thoughtfully facing each other in their treetop hideaway for a few moments before Darius spoke.

"Well, the drawings—and your vision, Delta—confirm that the turtle was a sacred Native American relic. And your vision proves that it's a powerful amulet. But if the turtle gave you a vision right there in the shell ring, and you saw the girls get those amulets in that very spot, what makes you so sure it's the wrong place?"

Delta raised both arms toward the sky. "Because everything is still going wrong! You said yourself that just because something has *been* at a certain place doesn't mean it *belongs* there."

"True." Darius nodded. "What do you think, Jax?"

"Well, I think since I found the turtle, it's totally unfair that it gave Delta a vision and not me. I mean, what the heck?"

Delta rolled her eyes, but Darius chuckled. The trio sat in silence for a moment in the aerie of the giant live oak.

"The bottom line is that burying the amulet where we did didn't break the curse," Darius said. "We've got to dig it back up and figure out another plan. Deal?" He held his fist out to his friends.

"Deal," Delta said, grabbing Darius' balled hand.

Jax shrugged and put his hand over both of theirs. "Deal."

Back at Darius' dock on Hilton Head, Delta and Jax waited while he tied up his boat.

Keisha and the cousins were nowhere to be seen as the trio slipped unnoticed into the graveyard, wound through the jungly path, and entered the shell ring. By daylight, Delta didn't find the site nearly as mysterious as she had the evening before. Even so, the contrast between this quiet, sunny glade and the crowded, busy version she had seen in her vision was stark.

The trio headed to the center of the ring and began searching for the amulet's burial plot.

"Remember? I put a palmetto frond on top to protect it," Darius said.

"That's right. Then here it is!" Jax triumphantly lifted a palm branch, only to reveal undisturbed ground beneath it. "Where'd it go?"

Delta glanced around the nearby vicinity and saw that at least a dozen palmetto fronds lay scattered throughout, most fallen from nearby trees. "Oh, brother."

The kids ran from frond to frond, picking up and tossing back down. Finally, Delta lifted a branch and discovered churned soil. "I found it! And in the last place we looked."

"Well, sure. Because now that we've found it, we can stop looking."

"Jax!" Delta laughed, digging in the loose, sandy earth with her bare hands. "Ta-da!" She lifted the pure white turtle from the ground, wiping stray soil from its shell. Jax took it from her and placed it carefully in the Velcroed pocket of his cargo shorts.

Heading toward the path that would lead them back to the graveyard and Darius' house beyond, the kids stopped to admire the view from the crumbling wall of shells on the edge of the marsh. For a moment, Delta thought she heard a girl's laughter, but no one was visible on the waters leading out to the Sound.

"Hey, do ya'll remember that girl that was laughing in the canoe last night, with the long dark hair?" Darius asked.

Did he just hear laughter again, too?

"I was just thinking about her," Delta said.

"Well, I remembered last night about this story that my granny—my dad's mother—used to tell sometimes. She called it 'The Legend of the Marsh Maiden.' She said there was this Native American girl who lived around here hundreds of years ago, but she died trying to save one of her friends from drowning. So, anyway, they say now her ghost guides lost travelers through area waters. I remember Granny saying she wasn't anything to be scared of. She was a happy ghost and laughed a lot."

"Huh." Delta smiled. "That's a nice story."

"Yeah," Darius said. "You don't suppose, I mean—"

Jax frowned. "We weren't lost on the water."

"No," Darius replied, "but we are kind of 'lost' and sure could use some help."

Delta stared out at the marsh, inhaling the pungency of the pluff mud. *Where's a friendly ghost when you need one?*

12

Driving on Base

"Ah-ah-CHOO!"

"Geez, Pops!" Jax wiped the sneeze from his arm. Delta was glad to be sitting by the passenger window of the truck, a bit farther away from her sniffling grandfather.

"Sorry about that, kiddos. This cold came upon me out of nowhere. I was fine last night, but this morning I'm feeling a bit under the weather."

The siblings shared a concerned look. First Tootsie had sprained her ankle, and now Pops was getting sick. They had to figure out how to break the turtle's curse before things got any worse.

Delta and her brother were accompanying Pops to Beaufort, where they would meet Mac and Darius at the Santa Elena Discovery Center.

They'd been driving for nearly an hour when the truck passed a green sign emblazoned with the words *Port Royal Sound*. They began climbing a long arched bridge, water spreading out in both directions as far as Delta could see. She noticed a flock of more than a dozen brown pelicans roosting on driftwood in the shallows of the Sound, taking in the morning sunshine. Farther out toward the open Atlantic Ocean, a shrimping boat spread its nets like a sea eagle ready to take flight.

"Hope you kids don't mind if we make a little detour. Since it was on our way, I offered to stop at Parris Island and pick up some artifacts for the Santa Elena Center."

"Native American stuff?" Jax asked.

"No, Mac's exhibit is something new. The Center's main focus is on Santa Elena itself. These items are from the archeological dig site."

Jax shrugged. "Who is Santa Elena anyway?"

"The Santa Elena *colony*, Jackson. Surely you learned about it in school?"

Delta and Jax both shook their heads and looked blankly at their grandfather.

"The Santa Elena colony was the capital of La Florida. Along with St. Augustine, it was one of the first European settlements in North America."

Delta shook her head. "Um, Pops. I'm pretty sure Tallahassee is the capital of Florida."

"That's right, Delta. But you're talking about the *state* of Florida. When Christopher Columbus sailed over in 1492—." Pops paused. "You've learned about *that*, haven't you?"

Pops' cold was making him grumpier than usual.

Jax rolled his eyes. "Duh!"

"Well, after Columbus found the New World, the country of Spain sent more explorers. When one of them—Ponce de León—landed in what we now call the state of Florida, he declared *all* of North America, as far as the land reached, the property of Spain. Because they saw a lot of flowering plants, they called the whole place the Spanish word for 'flowery'—*La Florida*."

"But wait," Jax said. "How could Spain just claim the whole continent for themselves? The pilgrims were from England, and they were living in Massachusetts when they had the first Thanksgiving, right?"

"The English didn't arrive at Plymouth until 1620," Pops explained. "The Spanish arrived more than one hundred years earlier."

"The Jamestown settlement in Virginia was before Plymouth, anyway," Delta added. "I learned that in school."

Pops nodded. "True, but that was still in the 1600s—1607, to be exact." When it came to history, Pops loved being exact. "Spain was settling the area around here half a century before that. You know, with your mother's Hispanic heritage, I'm surprised you kids don't already know about all this."

Delta shrugged. "Mom's grandparents were born in Cuba, Pops. Not Spain."

"Yes, but their ancestors were Spanish. Anyway, Spanish explorers built a fort at St. Augustine, where they first landed, and then headed north to establish a permanent colony right here on Port Royal Sound—on Parris Island. They built the town of Santa Elena in 1566 and declared it the capital of La Florida."

Pops veered the pickup truck off the main road and across a narrow, palm-edged causeway bordered on both sides by tidal marsh. The land bridge ended on an island, where a metal sign declared *U.S. Marine Corps Recruit Depot.*

"Um, Pops? Did we take a wrong turn?" Delta asked.

Pops smiled as the truck approached a barricaded guard gate.

"Sir, I'm going to have to see some identification."

"Of course, of course," Pops said, fumbling in his wallet for his driver's license. He handed the piece of laminated paper through the truck window.

"And proof of insurance for your vehicle."

"Delta, hand me the red plastic envelope in the glove compartment, please."

The uniformed guard examined both documents. Pops explained to the man that he had a meeting with Sergeant Heather Rodriquez. The sentry nodded, then checked a computer monitor mounted on the wall of the guard station. Finally, he turned back to the truck and returned Pops' papers, along with a map.

"Everything checks out, sir. Sergeant Rodriquez is waiting for you at the excavation site, which I've circled on the map for you. Welcome to Parris Island."

Delta waited until they were out of earshot of the guard. "What are we doing on a Marine base, Pops? I thought we were stopping at a dig site."

"We are. The original Santa Elena colony was right here on Parris Island, which is now a training camp for new Marine recruits."

Delta rode wide-eyed through the streets of the military base past brick office buildings, a health clinic, and a tree-shaded park scattered with picnic tables. At one intersection, a banner stretched across the street proclaiming WE MAKE MARINES.

"Whoa! Look at them!" Jax pointed to a line of young men and women in green and brown camouflaged uniforms, swinging their arms in unison as they marched across a grassy field.

"LEFT, LEFT, LEFT, RIGHT, LEFT," Delta heard them chant.

Farther down the street, a larger platoon of Marine recruits stood in formation, chanting something Delta couldn't quite make out through the closed truck window. Around them, trios of rifles were propped like miniature teepees.

"SIR, YES, SIR!" they suddenly shouted to their officer.

Referring to the map the gate guard had handed him, Pops turned at the next streetlight. Driving down a long, twisting lane flanked by towering pines, the trio left the commotion of the training area behind. Soon, the tall trees were replaced with rolling fields of sod.

"FORE!"

A white ball came whizzing by, and Delta saw two golf carts drive toward them.

"A golf course?" Jax asked.

Pops chuckled. "Why not? Marines like to play golf, too."

Delta admired a hefty alligator sunbathing on the bank of a lagoon, oblivious to the foursome playing a game nearby. She knew that gators were generally passive if you left them alone. Even so, she was happy to view this one from the safety of the truck.

Pops drove by the golf course clubhouse and to the end of the paved road before parking the pickup on the edge of Port Royal Sound. Across a grassy field, at the base of a tall white-painted water tower, a young woman in camouflaged pants and a Marines T-shirt looked up at them and waved.

"That must be her," Pops said, blowing his nose into a handkerchief. "Pardon my cold," he said as Sergeant Rodriquez approached.

The young woman smiled. "No problem, but I hope you don't mind if we skip the handshake."

The group introduced themselves, and the officer explained that she had been helping archaeologists from the University of South Carolina with the excavation. She led the way across the grass, which she said had previously been part of the golf course. Beyond it, a large area near the shoreline resembled a construction site. Pits of various depths pockmarked the field, with dozens of colored flags stuck into the ground to mark significant points of study.

"So, this was Santa Elena?" Jax asked.

"That's right," the Marine told him. "We've identified a number of buildings and continue to find Spanish artifacts. Your grandfather is going to take some of them to Beaufort for us so they can be displayed."

"Can you believe these kids had never even heard of the Santa Elena colony?" Pops asked her. "Apparently their school curriculum up in Chicago doesn't mention it."

Sergeant Rodriquez shrugged. "Actually, that doesn't surprise me at all. The history books usually mention Spanish explorers at St. Augustine in Florida, but the existence of Santa Elena had been virtually forgotten on our side of the Atlantic until about fifty years ago. Archeologists here initially thought they were excavating a French fort until they started finding so many Spanish artifacts."

"Then how'd they figure out the real story?" Delta asked.

"Someone had the idea to check historical records in Spain," the Marine said. "The colonists had sent detailed information on their settlement back to the Spanish king. Over time, though, those records had been locked away and forgotten. No one remembered the capital of La Florida anymore. In fact, you'll see in some outdated history books that St. Augustine was always the capital of La Florida, but we know now that just wasn't so."

Jax scowled. "So, history changed?"

"Our *understanding* of history changed," Pops said. "Happens all the time. We learn new things every day to help complete the story."

As Pops and Sergeant Rodriquez bent to examine a dig site, Delta and Jax roamed the seaside area that was apparently once the home of Spanish soldiers and settlers.

"Hey, Delta! There's another diving boat." Jax pointed out across the water, where a boat with a red flag rocked on the shimmering waves.

"That's not another diving boat, goofball. It's the same one we keep seeing from our beach on Hilton Head—just from the other side of Port Royal Sound. See the land behind it? That's Hilton Head Island. We just drove around the Sound to get over here."

"Huh." Jax stood looking over at the island they'd called home this summer, absentmindedly rolling the turtle amulet in his palm. "Ow!" he said suddenly, and dropped the carving onto the sandy ground.

"Watch it, Jax!" Delta whispered, glancing over her shoulder to ensure that Pops wasn't watching. "You're going to lose that thing before we have a chance to break the curse."

She leaned down to pick up the turtle, but Jax prevented that by grabbing her wrist.

"No, I'm not. It's just that it got hot all of a sudden." Still holding his sister's arm, Jax seized the amulet.

"Hot?"

It was the last word Delta spoke before fog engulfed them both.

13

Stepping through Time

Delta and Jax still stood looking out toward Port Royal Sound, with Hilton Head Island visible in the distance. The fog had cleared, but the boat had disappeared.

"Delta, what happened? Where's the diving boat? Omigosh! Did it sink?"

Delta knew better. She slowly turned to see where Pops and Sergeant Rodriquez had just been consulting over a dig site. She gulped as she saw, in their place, a small wooden structure with a peaked roof and openings for windows. The scene looked vaguely reminiscent of an old Wild West town she'd seen in so many cowboy movies. Two dozen plain pine buildings with palm-thatched roofs lined both sides of a sandy roadway leading to the water—a roadway on which she and Jax were now standing.

"It happened again," Delta whispered.

Jax wrapped both arms around his sister's elbow. "Is this the Indian village?"

"No, I think this is Santa Elena."

CLANG!

Both kids jumped and spun to see a man in a long woolen robe standing next to a large iron bell just feet away from them. On his signal, men, women, and children filed out of the wooden building behind him, some clutching crosses attached to strings of round glass beads.

"I think that's their church," Jax whispered.

Delta nodded. As in her other vision, these people seemed oblivious to the presence of strangers in their midst. They walked right past Delta and Jax as if the siblings were not even there.

"They can't see us," she said. "It's like we're ghosts or something."

"But I thought ghosts came from the past, not the future."

Delta shrugged and watched a family with two small children enter the house where Pops and his new Marine friend had been standing just a few minutes earlier. Their church service apparently complete, the colonists were now returning to their regular routines. Like the other men in the settlement, the leader of this household wore poofy, knee-length pants and long stockings, leather shoes, and a laced-up shirt. Although he wore a leather coat when he entered the building, Delta noticed he had shed it before coming back outside a moment later. He headed to an open-sided enclosure next to the house, where Delta saw him stoke a fire with a long metal prod and then stick a piece of black metal into the fire with a pair of tongs. When it had begun to glow red, the man retrieved the metal and hammered it flat with an iron mallet.

BOOM!

The sound of the blacksmith striking metal to metal was drowned out by the explosion of a cannon on the shoreline. Once again, the siblings spun in unison, Jax still clutching his sister's arm.

"Who are they shooting at?" he asked.

Delta scanned the waters of Port Royal Sound but saw no apparent targets. Three metal-helmeted men stood next to one of several cannons lined up facing the open sea. She watched as one pounded a black powder into the neck of the cannon with a stick that looked like a giant ear swab. Then another dropped in a metal ball about the size of a grapefruit. The third man lit the fuse and, as all three held their hands over their ears. Delta and Jax did the same.

"*¡Para España!*" the first man shouted.

BOOM!

One by one, the men tested each cannon on the beach.

"The other people in the village don't even seem to notice when they do that," Jax said.

"Maybe they do it every day, so it's no big deal."

"Sweet! I shot arrows at Boy Scout camp, but not with one of those." Delta followed her brother's pointing hand and saw two men firing arrows at a target with crossbows crafted from wood and iron. They hit the bullseye with nearly every shot.

Just then, a tall, bearded man wearing an elaborately stitched woolen jacket strode toward the shore. A woman in a brilliant blue satin gown, the gray-streaked hair braided atop her head pinned in place with ivory combs, walked beside him, her arm looped through his. The villagers bowed their heads at the couple as they passed, some speaking in a language that sounded oddly familiar to Delta.

"Who are they?" Jax asked.

Delta shook her head and observed the woman curtsy to the man before walking with another, more plainly dressed woman across the grass toward a larger building set apart from the others. Beds of yellow and red flowers sprouted beneath the glass windows that flanked each side of the home's front door.

Turning back to the tall man now standing on the shore of Port Royal Sound, so close that she could have reached out and touched him, Delta noticed sad eyes as he lifted something from inside his coat. She thought it was a gold pocket watch at first, since he opened it like she had seen Pops do with an antique watch he had inherited from his own grandfather. When the Spanish man held the item up, though, she saw that it was a hinged frame. The left side held a small portrait of the woman who had just accompanied him. The other side, the one the man gazed at as he sighed and discreetly wiped a tear from his eye, held a drawing of a young man with reddish hair and a freckled face.

"Hey! I know that guy," Delta said, grabbing her brother's arm as the fog rolled in.

Seeing the diving boat once again in its place in the Sound, Delta wasn't surprised when she turned to find Pops and Sergeant Rodriquez still deep in conversation. While she and Jax had experienced several minutes in the long-ago Santa Elena colony, she suspected that only a few seconds had passed here on present-day Parris Island—not enough time for the adults to notice anything strange, at any rate. She eyed her surroundings with a sigh. The wooden buildings of the Spanish settlement were gone, and now patterns of post holes and the charred remains of ancient hearths were the only indications of what had once been.

"Delta! Can you believe what just happened? I mean, you saw it, too, right?" Jax whispered.

"Shh. We'll talk about it later." Delta nodded toward Pops, who was motioning for them to join him.

"Mac's expecting us over in Beaufort," he called to them. "We should get a move on."

Pops picked up the box he was to transport to the Santa Elena Center, and the group headed to the truck. As they walked through the undisturbed grass of the former Parris Island golf course, though, Delta realized they were passing right over the site of the fancy Spanish woman's home.

"You might want to dig right here," she told Sergeant Rodriquez. "I mean, it looks like it would've been a great spot for a building of some sort."

The officer stopped and surveyed the area.

"You think so? I've wondered what this space might have been used for. I'll have to mention it to the archaeologists from the university and see what they think."

During the short drive to Beaufort, Delta couldn't stop considering the hundreds—no *thousands*—of people who had likely played golf right on top of the big Spanish colonial house. None of them had any inkling that, nearly five hundred years ago, red and yellow flowers had waved in the breeze beneath glass windows at the home of the elegant lady and her sad husband.

The portrait! Delta had nearly forgotten. She had recognized the young man depicted in the gold hinged frame. She had seen his freckled face in the Native American village on Hilton Head Island. *But what's his connection to the tall, bearded man at Santa Elena, and why did his portrait make the man so sad?* The turtle amulet had shown her all these things. *But what does this all have to do with breaking the turtle's curse?*

14

Handling a Bone

"What is this place, Pops?"

"It's the Santa Elena Discovery Center, Jackson. You knew we were coming here."

"No, I guess I mean, what *was* this place?"

Before them stood a gray stucco fort, its notch-topped walls towering about ten feet above Delta's head. A sturdy wrought-iron gate stood open in the single entryway, welcoming them into the Center's courtyard.

Pops sneezed twice before answering. "Long before it was a museum, this building was used as an arsenal for storing the town's ammunition."

"Like guns?" Delta asked.

Pops nodded. "Guns, cannons, gunpowder."

"Geez! Why does this town need that stuff?" Jax asked.

"It doesn't anymore," Pops chuckled. "That's why the space is used for something else now. But about a hundred fifty years ago, during the Civil War, the Beaufort Volunteer Artillery kept their weapons and supplies here."

Pops led the way through the gate, but Delta and Jax stopped dead in their tracks when they saw the courtyard's interior. As if stepping back inside their earlier apparition, the kids stared upon a lane of simple pine houses with palmetto-thatched roofs. Two men in knee-

length pants and metal conquistador helmets stood polishing a pair
of crossbows. Across the yard, another man in a black leather apron
hammered at a metal rod glowing red over an open fire.

Jax turned to his sister. "What the heck?"

"This is the living history portion of the Santa Elena Center," Pops
explained. "These reenactors are demonstrating what daily life was like for
the Spanish colonists. Almost feels like we're really back there, doesn't it?"

Delta gulped. "Almost."

Beyond the courtyard, a large rectangular building contained the
Center's indoor displays. Pops stopped by the front desk to drop off
the box of artifacts from Parris Island.

"Is Mac McGee around?" he asked the woman posted at the desk.

"Sure is. Second room on the left."

Following Pops down the hallway, Delta glanced into the first
display room they passed and did a double take. She waited until her
grandfather was a distance ahead of them, then grabbed her brother's
arm and pulled him into the doorway.

"It's *him,* Jax!" Staring straight at them was a life-sized statue of a
tall, bearded man in formal Spanish colonial clothing. There was no
mistaking it; he was the same man they had just seen looking so sad
at Santa Elena.

"No way!" Jax said, approaching the sculpture and looking up into
his face. "How could we have known there was somebody who looked
exactly like this?"

"It's the turtle. The same thing happened when I watched that chief
and her daughters in the shell ring, and then Mac had that drawing
of those very same people. I swear—that turtle amulet has some kind
of crazy magic that keeps sending us back in time to *real* places, and
we're seeing *real* people."

Jax leaned over a plaque at the base of the statue. "It says here
that this guy was Pedro Menéndez de Avilés. He established the Santa
Elena colony in 1566, and served as the governor of La Florida until
his death in 1574."

Delta couldn't stop staring at his familiar face. "The governor. That makes sense why his family would have a bigger, fancier house."

Glancing around the room now, she saw a weathered map titled *La Florida, 1568.* Without the benefit of satellite photos to tell them what North America really looked like, whoever had drawn this image had likely relied on little more than compass readings and explorer's descriptions of the new land.

"Look how weird this is, Jax. I mean, you can kind of tell what it's supposed to be, but the shapes are all a bit off. See, there's the state of Florida." Delta pointed to a distinct peninsula extending into a body of water labeled *Atlántico*—the Atlantic Ocean. Below it, a cluster of islands floated in the sea. "Hey—Cuba! Looks like the Spaniards settled there, too, just like Pops said."

Tracing her finger northward up the coast, Delta found *Presidio of San Agustin* right where the Florida city of St. Augustine is now. A few inches above that on the map, she saw *Santa Elena*—the colonial village she and her brother had so recently seen firsthand.

"Hey!" Jax called from a nearby poster. "I think I know why Pedro was so sad when we saw him."

"Don't call him that."

"Whatever. It says here that one of the reasons Señor Menéndez agreed to come to the New World from Spain was to look for his lost son."

"What?" Delta rushed to her brother's side. Sure enough, the poster described how Menéndez's only son, Juan, had been shipwrecked during an earlier expedition to La Florida and was never found. The father hoped to find his missing heir while establishing Spain's rights to the North American continent.

"But I know where he is," Delta said. "The lost son, I mean. I found him!"

"Quiet! Here comes Pops," Jax whispered.

"Where'd you kids go?"

"Coming, Pops!"

Mac was already hard at work when Delta and Jax stepped into the First Carolinians exhibit. Each corner of the room held a curved, glass-fronted display case, rounding the shape of the room so that the two-foot-high wall of oyster shells around the perimeter created a perfect shell ring.

"Wow! Where'd you get all those oysters?"

Mac laughed. "There aren't as many as it seems. We built an artificial barrier out of papier-mâché, and we're hot-gluing shells to the surface of it. Darius has been a big help with that."

Delta looked over to see her friend kneeling by a box of bleached shells. He smiled and waved, a glue gun in his hand.

"Where'd you get them, though?" Jax persisted.

"A lot of towns around here have recycling stations where restaurants and individuals can drop off empty shells," Mac said. "The Department of Natural Resources uses them to make artificial reefs so new oysters have a place to grow. I guess I'm going kind of old school using them for a shell ring."

Delta took in the rest of the room. The far wall held a large flat-screen television, while framed posters lined the others. Native American clothing hung in one of the corner cabinets, although the other three stood empty.

"These are some of the artifacts I was talking to you about," Mac said.

Pops leaned over a folding table his friend had set up in the center of the room. An assortment of tools, fabrics, and jewelry lay scattered atop the temporary workbench. As the men debated display options for the items, Delta and Jax examined the collected treasures.

"This one kind of reminds me of you know what," Jax whispered, nodding toward an eagle pendant strung onto a necklace of multicolored glass beads. The distinct shapes of tiny feathers had been intricately carved into the back of the pure white bird.

Noticing their interest, Mac lifted the eagle in his white-gloved hand and tilted it toward them for a closer look. "She's a beauty, isn't she?"

Delta nodded. "What kind of stone is that? I mean, it looks like a tiny marble statue, but marble doesn't come from around here, does it?"

Mac smiled. "Aha! You're right about marble not being a native stone. Early tribes carved this type of charm out of something native to these parts, but it wasn't stone at all. What else do you suppose it could have been?"

Mac's eyes twinkled as he looked from Delta's confused face to her brother's.

"Not stone . . . seashells?" Delta suggested.

"Good guess, but no. What else was there plenty of?"

"Um, plants? Trees and stuff. But that doesn't look like it's carved out of wood."

Mac smiled. "Right again. Not carved out of wood." He held the bird up toward the fluorescent ceiling light, illuminating its widespread wings. "Like many Native American carvings of that era, this baby's made out of bone."

"Bone? Like human bone?" Jax said, wide-eyed.

"Animal bone. The Native Americans weren't wasteful. They would use an animal's meat for food, its skin for clothing and shelter, and its bones for tools and jewelry. It polished up beautifully, don't you think?"

Delta agreed that it had, but she couldn't help but glance at her brother. Although he had found a lovely carving of a loggerhead sea turtle, the truth of the matter was that Jax had been carrying a chunk of dead animal bone around in his pocket. She shuddered, recalling that she, too, had handled the amulet. Bones creeped her out.

"Ouch!" Darius touched his index finger to his lips. "Man, this glue's hot! That's the second burn I've gotten since y'all got here."

Since the cursed turtle got here, Delta thought.

"Sounds like time you take a break, D.," Mac told his son, who was still sucking on his burnt finger. "Your mama always packs enough lunch to share, so why don't you kids head over to the park for a picnic."

"That sounds perfect," Delta said. She had a lot to discuss with Darius and Jax. The three kids had only gotten as far as the front desk of the Center, though, when a tanned man wearing a tropical shirt and sunglasses entered, scrolling through his cell phone.

"I'd like to speak with a representative of the museum about some artifacts," he told the attendant, not lifting his eyes from the phone. "I don't suppose you're authorized to make purchases?"

"No, sir, I'm afraid not."

"So, who's in charge here?"

"Well, there's a board of directors, but most days we're staffed by volunteers like me."

"Can I be of assistance?" Mac had apparently heard the commotion from all the way in the back of the building. The sunglassed man dropped the phone into his shirt pocket and looked up.

"I'm Jack Strader, of Treasures Unlimited. You may have noticed our boat out on Port Royal Sound."

"Oh! You're the diving guy," Jax said.

"That's right, kid. We've found some pretty great stuff out there and thought we'd give the Santa Elena Center first dibs on buying it."

Pops approached the group. "What types of things are you finding?"

"Cannons, coins, pottery. You name it. We've been staking out this wreck for a couple of years, and it's really paying off. We heard about the Santa Elena Discovery Center, though, and figured you might want to keep the swag around here."

"Well, since this facility is a not-for-profit organization, most of the artifacts displayed here are given to the museum as gifts," Mac said. "I don't suppose you'd be willing to donate some of the items you've discovered?"

Strader laughed loudly. "You're joking, right?"

"No, sir, I'm not. If you're discovering items of historical relevance to this area, I'm sure the Center here would love to display them. You could write off the donated items as a tax deduction."

"Not likely. We're in the diving business to make money, and if this place doesn't want to pay, there'll be plenty of collectors that will. Your loss." The treasure hunter pulled out his phone and was scrolling through it again as he exited the building.

Pops shook his head and sighed. "Folks like him have no respect for the true value of the treasures they're finding."

Mac agreed. "I just hope those relics end up in a museum where people can see them and not locked away in some private collector's closet."

Or in some kid's pocket, Delta thought, with a pang of guilt.

15

Swinging for Lunch

The three kids were seated in a porch swing suspended from a vine-covered arbor. From this spot in the waterfront park, they faced a broad bend in the Beaufort River, its harbor filled with bobbing yachts and sailboats. On the opposite bank, a dense pine forest crowded the shore. A metal bridge spanned the river just upstream from where they sat eating the pulled pork sandwiches Ruby had packed to share. Behind them the town's historical main street offered several blocks of quaint shops and restaurants.

"Darius, has your dad always worked in museums?"

"No, this is actually a first for him." Darius swallowed a large bite of bar-b-que before continuing.

"Dad's college degree is in Native American studies, and he volunteers all the time with the Tribal Council. But, jobwise, he's worked for the family restaurant ever since he and Mama got married about twenty-five years ago."

Delta took a swig from a can of soda. "So how'd he end up doing the First Carolinians thing?"

"Like I said, he's always had a passion for our Native American culture. The leaders of the Tribal Council knew that teaching others about our people was kind of a bucket list item for my dad, so they asked him to organize the exhibit."

Darius crunched a handful of potato chips, gazing out at the river, its sun-splashed surface sparkling as if bedazzled with sequins. Then he turned to Delta and Jax. "You know, my dad's always been a jolly enough guy, I guess. But since he's started doing this project, I've never seen him happier. It's his dream job, really, and it's been exciting for our whole family to have *him* so excited."

Delta nodded as if she understood, but she felt a rock hit the pit of her stomach. Weren't her own parents excited about the chance to fulfill their dreams? As a geologist, Mom had been passionate about meteorites for, well, forever. Delta remembered once, as a kindergartner, bringing a small meteorite sample from Mom's collection for show-and-tell. While the other kids thought the metallic rock was awesome, their excitement had paled compared to Mom's delight in sharing it with Delta. And now she had the chance to lead her own expedition to one of the best places on earth to find fallen stars.

And what about Dad? He was a great photographer, but he did sometimes complain that taking pictures of government officials and city events for the newspaper got tedious. The nature photos he took for fun were always gorgeous and, more important, taking them seemed to make him happy. Wouldn't photographing scenery in the wilds of the Arctic Circle be an adventure for him? Maybe he and Mom could turn this opportunity into a magazine article in one of the nature magazines they both loved so much. Delta had to admit, as much as she and Jax hated the idea, this Siberia thing could be life-changing for their parents.

"Again? Both of you? Delta, is Jax making this up?"

"Huh?"

"Jax said y'all *both* had a vision over at the Santa Elena dig site. For real?"

Delta snapped back from her thoughts of Siberia and once again found herself swinging on the banks of the Beaufort River. "Oh! No, I swear it really happened. Jax was holding the turtle, and it got hot, so he dropped it. But then, he grabbed me and the turtle at the same time, and—"

"And this weird fog was all around us! Did you see that, too, Delta?"

"Yes, and then when it cleared we were standing in the same spot, except hundreds of years ago!"

Jax's eyes were wide. "I saw houses, and a bunch of people came out of this church, and a guy was a blacksmith—"

"And we saw Pedro Menéndez!" Delta said.

"Who?" Darius asked.

"Pedro Menéndez," Jax replied. "We found out later, at the Santa Elena Discovery Center, that he was the governor of La Florida. Did you know Santa Elena was the capital of the whole continent back then?"

Darius shook his head.

"We didn't know who the man was when we first saw him," Delta explained. "He was dressed kind of fancy, and everybody sort of bowed at him as he passed, so we figured he must be somebody important."

"And his house was bigger than everyone else's," Jax added.

Delta nodded. "Right. But he looked so sad. And then he came and stood right by us, and he was looking at this little gold frame."

"I even saw him cry a little bit," Jax said.

"Yes, but the thing is, I recognized the portrait he was looking at. I've seen that guy before."

"What? Who was it?"

"Darius, the exhibit at the center said that Pedro Menéndez came to La Florida not just to establish a colony but also to look for his son, who had been lost in a shipwreck over here somewhere."

"But he never found him," Jax said.

"That's just it," Delta grinned. "*I* found him. I know where the Lost Son is. Or was."

"How could you know that?" Darius asked.

"The guy in the portrait Pedro Menéndez was holding at Santa Elena—I saw that same guy when I was in the shell ring village. He was laughing with one of the princesses. Remember, didn't I tell you I saw a young man with freckles and reddish hair wearing weird clothes? Well, different from the Native Americans anyway. I'm *positive* it was the same guy."

Darius pushed his glasses higher on his nose as he considered what Delta and Jax had just told him. "So, the governor of La Florida was living at Santa Elena, and his missing son was just a few miles away living with a Native American tribe. And they never found each other?"

Delta shook her head. "Apparently not, because the museum display still refers to him as the 'Lost Son'."

"So, *nobody* found him," Darius clarified.

Jax scrunched his face. "But then whatever happened to him? I mean, they were so close to each other."

Darius shrugged. "Maybe he just wanted to live forever with the tribe, Jax."

"Or maybe he ended up marrying one of the princesses with the turtle amulets," Delta said.

Jax pulled the white carving from his pocket and held it up to the sunlight. A pinpoint of light shone through the hole at the turtle's neck, an opening Delta now realized had been created to hold a necklace.

"What kind of bone do you suppose they used to make this?" he asked.

Darius reached over to take the amulet for a closer look. He turned it over in his hand, examining the intricate carved pattern on the animal's shell.

"Hard to know for sure, but I suppose it could have been from a loggerhead. I mean, that would make sense. A shoulder bone or a skull would've been big enough."

Delta shuddered. "That's so gross."

The kids sat swaying on the porch swing overlooking the harbor. Nibbling on Miss Ruby's yummy sandwich, Delta basked in the warmth of the sun on her face, relishing these last days of summer and the familiar Lowcountry environment. Curse or no curse, just for now she was going to pretend things were okay. Her momentary peace was broken, though, when a movement on the metal bridge spanning the river suddenly caught her eye.

"Omigosh! The bridge is breaking!" she cried.

Darius laughed at Delta's confusion. "That's the swing bridge to Lady's Island. It's like a drawbridge, except instead of raising up, the center of it swings at a ninety-degree angle to let tall boats through."

Sure enough, Delta noticed a sailboat, its sails furled, approaching the crossing. The center portion of the bridge continued to turn until it hung parallel with the flow of the river.

"What if somebody was driving on that bridge when it swung like that, Darius? They'd drive right off the edge and into the river."

"No, Jax, they stop traffic before they swing it."

The trio watched the sailboat move ever closer to the gap left by the twisted bridge. Still holding the amulet, Darius lifted it to his face. He closed one eye and held the hole in the turtle's neck up to the other, pressing the bone up against the lens of his glasses.

"Hey, it's like a telescope, except things don't look any closer," he laughed.

Delta and Jax chuckled along, but all three kids jumped up when the mast of the sailboat smashed into the metal bridge railing.

"Oh no!"

Delta and Jax stared toward the accident site, watching the boat slow its pace as its mast scraped along the side of the structure.

"Nobody move!" Darius cried.

Delta looked down to see her friend on his hands and knees in the grass beneath the porch swing. "What are you doing?"

"I jumped up so fast, my glasses fell off." He crawled on the ground, waving his hands back and forth on the sod around him.

"You dropped the carving, too." Before Delta could stop him, Jax had taken a step toward the cursed turtle. As he reached for his discovery, though, all three kids heard the crunch of glass.

Darius groaned. "Everywhere that turtle goes, bad things happen."

"We have *got* to figure out what it's trying to tell us," Delta said. "We have to break its curse before anything else goes wrong!"

16

Making a Choice

Jax had popped his head into Delta's room as she finished making up the daybed the next morning. He stood leaning against the doorframe, his arms crossed and his eyes rolling.

"Get ready to hear how fun it'll be living in an igloo."

"What are you talking about?"

"Mom's on the phone. Pops is talking to her right now."

"Listen, Jax. I was thinking yesterday, when Darius was saying how excited his family is about Mac getting his dream job—you know, this Siberia thing is our parents' dream."

"So now you *want* to live at the North Pole?"

"Of course not. And it isn't exactly the North Pole. Anyway, it just made me feel kind of guilty, that's all. Maybe we're being selfish about moving."

"I don't care so much about moving, Delta. Not in general. There are probably lots of fun places to live. But where Mom and Dad want to go, there won't be a house, internet, friends, or even school."

"I'd have thought you'd consider that last one a plus."

Jax shrugged. "Some things about school are fun."

Delta headed toward the kitchen, where Pops handed her the telephone. "Hey, Mom."

"Hi, sweetie. Pops was just telling me that storm out in the Atlantic is getting worse. Sounds like you might end up having to evacuate the island in the next couple of days. You and your brother be good and don't cause your grandparents any extra worry, okay? This will be hard enough as it is, with Pops sick and Tootsie on crutches."

Delta glanced into the living room where Tootsie was hobbling toward a chair. "We'll be good."

"Sweetie, another reason I called was that your Dad and I have been talking. Is your brother there? He should hear this, too."

Delta waved Jax to the phone and then held the receiver out so they could both listen to their mother.

"Hi, Mom."

"Hi, Jax. So, as I was saying, as excited as we are about this Arctic Circle expedition, family comes first. If you two aren't on board with the idea, Dad and I think we should take a pass on it."

Delta looked at her brother, and the siblings shared a grin. *Too good to be true! Isn't it?*

"But what about your jobs?" she asked.

"I guess we'll just keep doing what we've been doing. It'll be fine."

The disappointment in Mom's voice was clear and such a contrast to the enthusiasm they'd heard from her and Dad during their last couple of conversations. Delta swallowed the lump in her throat. The prospect of moving halfway around the world terrified her, but she knew what had to be done.

"No, Mom. I think you should accept the offer. I mean, it's a once-in-a-lifetime opportunity, right?"

Jax shoved Delta's shoulder so hard it nearly knocked her off balance. She shot him a stern look.

"What about you, Jax?"

"Well, geez, Mom. Are you *sure* there isn't Boy Scouts there?"

"Pretty sure, buddy."

He took a deep breath before responding. "No, you should do it. Once-in-a-lifetime and all that."

Delta patted her brother on the back. She knew he didn't want to move to Siberia any more than she did, but she also knew it was the right move for Mom and Dad.

"Oh, you two are the best kids any parents could ever ask for! And we'll make it a real adventure, I promise."

Pops, who had been brewing a pot of coffee throughout the conversation, coughed into his shoulder and reached out his hand for the phone. "Let me talk to her again."

Delta gave him the receiver and trudged into the living room with Jax. Tootsie had made it into the chair and was reading the morning newspaper, her crutches propped against the wall nearby. "Oh no! Two more vandalized turtle nests."

Jax scowled. "I just don't get why someone would do that."

"Neither do I, Jax," Tootsie said, shaking her head. "I wish I could get to the beach to see what's happening. I don't suppose I could do anything to help, really, but I just feel so out of the loop stuck in the house like this."

"We could go to the beach and check things out for you, if you'd like," Delta offered.

"Oh, would you, sweetie? That'd make me feel better about neglecting my Turtle Team duties."

"Sure, Tootsie. We'll get right on it."

"Thanks so much. But don't take too long. Pops needs your help at the Island History Museum this afternoon. We've got to start preparing for Hurricane Jackson."

17

Searching for Vandals

Port Royal Sound was churning beneath a sunny sky when the kids arrived at the beach. Waves taller than Jax crashed onto the sand, while white caps foamed in dancing peaks. Even so, Delta could see the boat with the red diving flag as it tossed wildly on the roiling waters.

"Over there." Jax pointed toward a cluster of beachgoers, several wearing the familiar orange shirts of the island's Turtle Team. The siblings plodded across the beach, their feet sinking into the powdery white sand with each step.

"Hey, what are y'all doing here?"

Delta turned to see their friend following along behind them.

"Probably the same thing you are, Darius—getting a firsthand look at the Nest Vandal's latest crime."

"You got new glasses," Jax said. "That was quick."

Darius shrugged and shoved the plastic nosepiece higher. "They're just my old pair. Mama says they'll have to do until we can get to the eye doctor after the storm passes."

The trio joined the gathering crowd and saw that, this time, two adjacent nests had been dug up. Once again, smooth round eggs lay scattered across the dunes, like a ping-pong game gone haywire.

"Excuse me! *Excuse me!*" A woman in high-heeled shoes and a yellow vinyl raincoat teetered through the soft sand, pushing spectators aside as she passed. Behind her, a man carried a large video camera on his shoulder.

"This spot right here," the woman told him, struggling to balance on the edge of one of the destroyed nests.

A man wearing a Turtle Team shirt stepped forward. "I'm sorry, ma'am, but you can't get that close to the nest. They're a protected species, you know, and—"

"I know all that," the woman said with a wave of her hand. "But this one's already messed up anyway, and this camera angle will be best."

"She's that reporter we keep seeing on TV," Delta said.

Up close, it was clear that Judy Drench was wearing heavy stage makeup, melting a bit in the August Lowcountry heat. She blotted her brow with a tissue and added an extra touch of bright pink lipstick as the cameraman positioned himself with his equipment.

"Wow! Her hair seems even bigger in person," Jax said.

The three kids stifled a giggle as the cameraman signaled a countdown with his fingers and the woman smiled widely and began to speak.

"Ladies and gentlemen, this is Judy Drench reporting live from Hilton Head Island. As Hurricane Jackson barrels directly toward us, landfall expected within forty-eight hours, I must report that the infamous Nest Vandal has struck yet again. This time, not just one, but *two* loggerhead turtle nests have been destroyed during the night as islanders peacefully slept, oblivious to the terrible crimes being committed right here in their own island paradise."

"Dramatic much?" Darius whispered.

"Excuse me, sir." Judy Drench reached out and grabbed the Turtle Team man by the arm and pulled him into the camera's view.

"You represent the Turtle People here on Hilton Head, is that correct?" She shoved her handheld microphone into the man's face.

"I'm a member of the Turtle Team."

"And what do you have to say about the continued sabotaging of these rare sea turtle nests?"

The man cleared his throat and spoke into the microphone. "Well, the nests themselves are not especially rare. There are several hundred of them here on the island this summer. But only a small percentage of the hatchlings survive to adulthood, making the species endangered."

"Yes, but what do you think of the scandalous wrongdoings being committed here? Some people are saying the Nest Vandal may represent an organized crime problem here on the island or perhaps government corruption. What do you think of that?"

Confused, the man scanned the crowd observing his interview. "Organized crime? Government corruption? Who's saying *that*?"

"So you're saying there is no criminal element on Hilton Head?"

"Um, no, not that I know of. We just want whomever, or whatever, is upsetting these loggerhead nests to stop. We—"

"Thank you, sir." The reporter gave the man a light shove out of the camera's angle. He stumbled a bit before finding his footing, still looking a bit dazed from the sensational questioning. She turned and grinned broadly into the camera.

"You heard it here first, ladies and gentlemen. A massive crime wave haunts this seemingly idyllic island, and Channel 1 News is on top of it. Stay tuned for the latest updates on the notorious Hilton Head Nest Vandal."

"Notorious?" Darius said. "The nests have only been messed with for the past few days. She's acting like the Nest Vandal is already world famous or something."

The kids watched as the reporter patted at her heavily sprayed hair, stiff even as the coastal wind picked up speed. In her struggle to stand upright, her spikey heels sinking into the soft sand, she grabbed a woman standing nearby. Startled, the woman jerked and Judy Drench nearly tumbled into the open hole of the disturbed nest.

"Hey, watch it, lady," the reporter snarled.

"Maybe if you weren't wearing high heels on the beach," the other woman said under her breath as she walked away.

"Hey, y'all, look! It's that treasure hunter guy we saw in Beaufort," Darius said.

Delta turned to see that one of the onlookers for the news report was Jack Strader, who was now having a heated discussion with a blonde woman in a Turtle Team shirt.

"How many times do we have to tell you?" the woman said. "You can't pile your artifacts right here on the beach. You're blocking the turtle nests." The woman waved her arm beyond the gathered crowd, where the kids now saw a long row of rusted metal tubes lined up above the high-tide line.

"The city of Hilton Head says we can, and so we will."

"I've seen a copy of your city permit, and it specifically states that you cannot place the items where they'll endanger wildlife. Hatchlings are not going to be able to get past that row of cannons to get to the water."

"Yeah, well, this town seems kind of obsessed with those little crustaceans, if you ask me," Strader replied with a laugh.

"Loggerheads are marine reptiles."

"Whatever. Just let me and my crew do our job. And if the Nest Vandal keeps doing *his* job, we won't have to worry about any more baby turtles hatching anyway. Am I right?"

The treasure hunter laughed again, to which the Turtle Team member groaned and threw up her hands. The kids watched her stomp back toward her fellow team members before returning their attention to Strader.

"Man, I'll be glad once those stupid nests are history," the man mumbled.

Delta, Jax, and Darius stared down at the first of about a dozen barnacle-covered cannons lined up on the beach. Wooden railroad ties lay perpendicular beneath them, creating a support to keep the metal from touching the sand. Ranging in length from three to eight feet, some of the old weapons were more corroded than others, but all were covered in a thick coat of rust.

"How old do you suppose these things are, Darius?"

"I'd say hundreds of years old. They could be from the time of the Spanish settlers, or maybe they're more recent, like from the Civil War. Lots of ships have sunk out in Port Royal Sound, you know."

The trio gazed out over the choppy waters and beyond.

"Look, guys! There's Santa Elena right over there, where the water tower is standing." Delta pointed to a spot on the opposite shore of the Sound. Funny how they could see the site of the former colony from their own beach, but it had taken them nearly an hour to drive around the Sound to Parris Island. From here, that entire island looked forested and wild. You'd never guess it held a modern Marine Corps base.

"Um, guys—" Jax said.

Delta turned to see her brother clutching the amulet he was now wearing on a leather cord around his neck. He had kept the turtle discreetly tucked under his T-shirt all morning, but now he had pulled it out and held it up so they could see its rosy glow.

"It's getting hot again, guys!"

Thinking fast, Delta grabbed Jax's arm with one hand and Darius' with the other.

"What the—" Before Darius could ask any questions, the waves crashing on the shore of Port Royal Sound were hidden by a strange and sudden fog.

18

Saving Some Friends

*B*OOM!

"What just happened?" Thunder clapped as Darius looked frantically around. The fog had receded to reveal clouds the color of charcoal over Port Royal Sound. Bolts of lightning bit the surface of the foaming waves as plump raindrops began to fall. "Boy, that came up fast."

Delta swallowed hard. "Um, Darius, I don't think this is when you think it is."

"Huh?"

Jax poked Darius in the shoulder and pointed to the trio's left. The row of rusty cannons had been replaced by a row of carved wooden canoes parked on the now-blowing sand.

"Wait!" Darius stared. "Where did those come from?"

"Welcome to the magic of the turtle," Jax said, spreading his arms wide.

Delta nodded. "It's been like this every time. The amulet gets hot, things get foggy, and then whoever has the turtle—or, I guess, is touching the person who has the turtle—gets transported or something. We're in the same place, just in a different time."

"But, Delta, how do we get back? To our own time, I mean?"

She shrugged. "It just sends us back whenever we've seen what it wants us to. At least, that's how it's happened so far."

Although Darius was startled, Delta and Jax watched calmly as a group of Native American men came running toward them on the beach.

"Don't worry. They can't see us," Jax said.

The men reached the canoes and began pushing them out into the crashing waves, shouting in words the kids didn't recognize. Delta wondered why they would risk the waters in the worsening storm, but then she saw their target. Far out in the middle of Port Royal Sound, where the diving boat had been bobbing all week, an old-fashioned sailing ship bent at an odd angle over the roller-coaster waves. She could just make out small figures falling from the ship's deck into the roiling sea below.

"Omigosh! Those people are going to drown!" Delta said.

"And the marsh tackies, too! Look!" Darius pointed to the left of the floundering vessel, where several horses struggled in their attempt to swim to shore.

"What were horses doing on a ship?" Jax asked.

Darius shrugged, his eyes fixed on the scene before them. "Maybe they were being delivered to the colony. It could be a supply ship."

Delta raised her hand in a salute to shield her face from the falling rain. She squinted to see Parris Island in the distance, but there was no water tower to mark the spot.

"I'd fall overboard for sure if I tried to paddle like that, even in calm water."

Jax motioned toward the fleet of canoes heading out into the deeper water toward the capsized ship. Every vessel was captained by a pair of men standing upright, digging their wooden paddles through the rough waters at a surprisingly swift speed. Delta watched the lead canoe approach a sailor struggling in the Sound and saw one of the tribal members reach down and pull the stranger into the craft.

"They're rescuing them!"

Thunder boomed again as another man ran toward the trio on the beach, followed by a maiden wearing a loggerhead amulet around her neck.

"Hey! Is that—?"

Delta nodded at Darius. The freckle-faced young man in the white lace-up shirt began to pull one of the canoes toward the surf. She knew now that he was Juan Menéndez, the Santa Elena governor's lost son. The kids watched as the Native American princess grabbed Juan's arm, firmly shaking her head from side to side. She clearly didn't want her friend to risk his life, but the lost son pointed to the sinking ship and tapped his own chest. Those were *his* people out there, and he was determined to help them.

Juan gently unwrapped the maiden's fingers from around his arm, kissed the back of her hand, and then dragged the canoe into the breaking waves. As he paddled toward his fellow Spaniards, the princess stood watching for a moment from the windswept shore, tears streaming down her face. Then she, too, hefted a canoe into the tossing sea and headed into the storm to save her friend.

As lightning flashed and rain poured from the darkening sky, rising fog engulfed the trio.

All three kids blinked into the midday sunshine. Although the waves on Port Royal Sound continued to toss wildly, the sinking Spanish galleon was no longer there. In its place, the familiar diving boat with its red flag bounced on the waters. Beyond it, the white Parris Island water tower marked the site of the colonists' home nearly five hundred years ago.

"How are we not wet?" Jax brushed at his arms as Darius shook his dark hair, expecting rain to fly from his head.

"Okay, y'all. I have a confession." Darius looked at his friends with guilty eyes. "When you told me about your visions, I thought those were pretty cool stories. I mean, I'm kind of superstitious, and I'm not saying there's *not* such things as magic or ghosts or whatever. But, time travel? Come on. That's kind of crazy talk! Or at least I thought that until just now."

"So you didn't believe us before?" Delta asked. "But you acted like you did."

Darius stared at his feet shuffling in the sand as he spoke. "I guess I *wanted* to believe you. Lots of bad stuff *has* been happening since you found that turtle amulet, and you did seem to know stuff you shouldn't have known. Or at least you *said* you did."

Jax scowled. "You must have thought we were just a couple of nutjobs."

"No, Jax," Delta said softly. "He thought we were a couple of little kids playing a game."

"I didn't think you were little kids, but, yeah, I maybe thought we were kind of playing a game. I wanted to play, too, though. I mean, y'all are great!"

"But we weren't just playing."

"I know that now, Jax. That's what I wanted to say. I'm sorry I didn't get it before. I don't know how it works, but that turtle really does have magical powers."

"This time it showed us that Juan Menéndez wanted to help the Spaniards," Delta said. "He didn't plan to just stay with the tribe."

Darius nodded. "True, but his father never did find him. I hate to say it, y'all, but I don't think Juan Menéndez made it through that storm."

Jax gazed in the direction of the water tower, where they had seen Pedro Menéndez stare sadly at the framed portrait of his only boy. "His dad never even knew how close he was to finding his lost son."

The kids were quiet as this truth sunk in. Delta thought of her own Spanish ancestors who, at some point, had braved the Atlantic Ocean in wooden ships in search of a new life in Cuba. Perhaps they'd lost family and friends in the process, too. Compared to what her forgotten family had likely endured, flying to Siberia in a comfy jet airplane didn't seem quite so bad.

Darius perked up. "Hey! I think I know who the girl on the beach is."

"Well, sure," Delta said. "She was that female chief's daughter—one of the three sisters. I saw her in my first vision, in the shell ring. And your dad had a drawing of her."

Darius grinned as he shook his head. "No, Delta. I don't mean who she *was*. I know who she is *now*."

19

Prepping for Disaster

Tiny live oak leaves swirled around them like gnats as Delta and Jax pedaled their bikes up the long, winding drive to the Island History Museum. The morning's breeze had morphed into gusts, and the twisted branches overhead scratched together as they bent to the coming storm's power.

OOMPH!

"Jax! You almost made me crash." Delta stood with one foot braced on each side of her bicycle, steadying the handlebars. She had nearly rammed into her brother when he had unexpectedly slammed on his brakes.

"Sorry," he said, turning toward her, his face hidden by a wad of Spanish moss. "It's really windy out here." He swiped the stringy plant onto the ground.

Delta burst out laughing. "That's Hurricane Jackson for you."

At the main museum building, the kids could see that Pops had already been hard at work preparing the site for the upcoming storm. The heavy wooden hurricane shutters were closed and latched over each of the old house's tall windows, and a sheet of plywood was nailed over the side entrance doorway. Pops met them on the wide front porch, where he was lifting a basket of dangling ferns from a hook in the ceiling.

"Hey, kiddos. Thanks for helping out. Could you please bring all these rocking chairs in for me? Just set them in the entry hall."

Delta and Jax each grabbed a chair by the arms and tottered toward the door. Between the three of them, the porch furniture and plants were cleared within ten minutes.

"We saw that treasure hunter guy down at the beach, Pops," Delta said as she helped store hanging ferns under a display table. "He had a bunch of old cannons lined up in the sand."

"Really? Well, he'd better get them moved before the hurricane hits. A tidal surge could wash them right back out to sea."

"A tidal surge?"

Pops nodded. "It's like a giant wave that hits the beach during a hurricane."

"Oh. Well, a Turtle Team lady wanted the cannons moved, too, because she said they were blocking the loggerhead nests. She told him the baby turtles wouldn't be able to crawl around them to reach the water."

"I imagine that's true," Pops said, placing a rocking chair against the wall.

"How old do you think those cannons are?"

Pops stopped to sneeze, then blew his nose loudly into a handkerchief before answering.

"I haven't seen the artifacts myself, but I know that ship they're diving on was a galleon bringing supplies to the Santa Elena colony from St. Augustine. The Spanish explorers kept detailed records, so we know she sunk in a hurricane in 1573."

Delta and Jax locked eyes. They had stood on the beach during that very hurricane, had watched that same galleon struggle in the roiling waters of Port Royal Sound.

"Well, kiddos, I need to turn the water off at the main valve. Since you did such a nice job with the rockers, why don't the two of you get the Adirondack chairs out back? Just put them in the toolshed, but make sure the door's latched shut when you're done."

The kids headed through what had once been a dining room in the old plantation house, passing familiar exhibits describing the nature and history of Hilton Head. Delta sighed as she spotted a favorite Civil War display about the Battle of Port Royal Sound, the deep anchorage where she had just stood a couple of hours ago. She'd learned so much about this island's secrets this summer and had come to feel like she belonged here. Could Siberia ever feel like home?

On the far side of the room, she opened the back door and slammed face-first into a sheet of plywood. "Ow! Are you kidding me?"

"I guess Pops already sealed that exit," Jax said with a giggle.

Delta rubbed her bumped nose. "Thanks, Captain Obvious."

Retracing their path, they went back out the front door and down the porch steps. Rounding the building to the back patio, they came upon four chairs circling a decorative fountain.

"I guess he got the water turned off." Delta and Jax watched as the fountain's powerful spout sputtered, shrank, and then disappeared. They attempted to lift the Adirondacks, which proved much heavier than the rockers had been, and then resorted to dragging them across the stone patio to a wooden toolshed. The old hinges squeaked as Jax swung the double doors open.

"How the heck are we supposed to fit them all in here?"

Delta stepped forward and rolled a lawnmower as far back as it would go, then rearranged a collection of garden tools until there was a clear spot barely big enough to fit the four chairs. She and Jax dragged and shoved until they could just squeeze the double doors together and force the latch closed. Returning to the front yard, they had to shield their faces from flying sand and crushed oyster shells ripped from the drive by the strengthening wind.

"Hello, there, Delta and Jax. Enjoying this fine weather?"

"Mac! What are you doing here?"

"We're getting the marsh tackies ready for the storm. Darius is over in the barn right now."

"Let's go," Jax said, but Delta had a question before they joined their friend.

"Mac, when we were at your house the other day, I saw a drawing of a Native American chief—a woman—who had three daughters. I was just wondering if you know anything else about them."

"Ah, the Legend of the Three Sisters."

"There's a legend about them? Because they were the daughters of a female chief?"

"No, actually female chiefs weren't all that rare. Many Native American tribes have had matriarchal societies, in fact. That means the women—the mothers and grandmothers—are the family leaders."

"But what about the three sisters?" Delta asked.

"That's what made these particular princesses so special—they were triplets. Natural triplets are rare even today, so when the tribe's chief gave birth to them, it was considered an omen. Their arrival was a blessing, and as long as the three sisters were together, their tribe prospered."

"As long as they were together?"

Mac nodded. "That's the sad part. One of the princesses disappeared during a storm, breaking the sisters' bond. From that point on, the tribe believed it was cursed. They suffered famine, caught deadly diseases, and the friendly relationship they'd had with the Spanish settlers in the area started to sour. Eventually, their numbers dwindled to nearly nothing, and the few survivors that remained had to go find other tribes to live with."

"Wow. That's awful," Delta said.

"Some people even believe the curse extended beyond the Native Americans to the Spanish settlers, too. Conflicts with the tribes, a lack of supplies, and some poor leadership after Pedro Menéndez died led the Spanish to abandon Santa Elena forever within about ten years or so of the princess's disappearance."

"Who knew one girl could make such a difference?" Jax said.

Mac smiled and winked at Delta. "Oh, never underestimate that. Anyway, that's the Legend of *Tso'i igido*."

"What's '*choy-ee-gee-doh*'?"

"That means *three sisters*, Jax. The tribe believed their people would continue to be cursed until the three sisters were reunited. As far as I know, that hasn't happened yet."

Delta looked at her brother. The turtle amulet hanging hidden beneath his T-shirt represented that curse—a curse now stronger than ever. The siblings turned toward the barn, Delta repeating Mac's strange words aloud. "*Choy-ee-gee-doh. Choy-ee-gee-doh.*"

Why did that phrase sound so familiar?

"Dad! Dad!" Darius ran toward them across the meadow at a full sprint. "Dad! I was putting Honey in her stall in the barn, and I swear I closed the gate! I *swear* I did!"

Mac met his son in the driveway and placed both hands on Darius' shoulders. "Calm down and take a deep breath, D. What's happened?"

Darius leaned forward, hands on his thighs, gulping air as he spoke. "I got Honey all settled in safe and sound in the barn. She should be fine during the storm. But then I went back outside to get Indigo, and the gate to the corral was ajar. He must've pushed it open or something, Dad."

"Is he alright?"

"That's just it. I don't know what happened to him. The hurricane is coming, and Indy is gone!"

After instructing the kids to search the museum grounds, Mac saddled Honeybee and rode off to check the surrounding neighborhoods for her runaway mate. With any luck, one of them would find the marsh tacky before he got too far away. Darius handed Delta and Jax each a handful of carrots from a bucket in the barn, hoping the treats might lure Indy back.

"We'll cover more space if we split up," Delta suggested, so the three friends scattered.

"Come on, Indigo! Here, boy!" Delta heard Darius shout from across the pasture. "I know you're spooked by the weather, buddy, but we've got to get you inside."

She turned from her search of the camellia garden, hoping Indy had trotted back to his owner, but Darius was calling in vain. There was no horse in sight. She could see Jax heading around the side of the main building. Perhaps he would have better luck.

Delta sighed. Good luck hadn't really been their "thing" lately.

About a half hour had passed when she came upon Darius by the kayak rack near the salt marsh. Sitting slumped on a fallen log, he seemed unaware of her presence.

"Hey, I told Pops what happened and he took his pickup to hunt for Indy."

Darius turned his head away, but she saw him wipe his cheek with the back of one hand. "Thanks."

Delta joined her friend on the log. "I'll bet he was just scared of all the wind and stuff, you know? He'll probably get tired of being outside and head back to the barn before long."

"I hope so."

"You said he's really smart, right? So he wouldn't want to stay out in a storm."

"I guess."

Delta stared out at the choppy waters of the salt marsh that lined one side of the museum property. The tide was high now, obscuring most of the fragrant pluff mud below. The wind blew puffs of foam up onto the shoreline. It occurred to Delta that the old shell ring lay just a few miles upstream.

"Hey! Do you think Indy would have gone to your house? He's only been staying here for a few days, so he might have run right up the road to get back home."

Darius shook his head. "No, we didn't keep him at our house. Before the museum, we boarded him and Honey at a farm over on Daufuskie Island. I'd take the ferry over there a few times a week to see him, but that's what was so great about moving him to your grandfather's museum on Hilton Head. I was going to get to be with him every day."

"Oh." Delta had exhausted all her optimism, so she sat on the log in silence. Several minutes passed before Darius spoke.

"See, the thing is, Indy is like my best friend. Don't tell anybody, but I don't have a lot of friends at school. And I know there are always tons of people around my house, but sometimes that just makes me feel kind of invisible, you know? Like, Micah and C.J. are really into sports and I'm kind of terrible at all that, and Keisha wants me to play little kid games. Mom and Dad are great, but they've always got their own stuff going on. I mean, I know Indy's not a person, but I can talk to him about anything, and he's a really great listener. He never judges me or expects anything of me. All he wants me to do is take care of him, and now I've let him down."

Darius turned his back to her and put his face in his hands. Delta gently placed a hand on his shaking shoulder.

"I'm sure he'll be back soon, Darius. Your dad and Pops are looking, and he's just bound to turn up. And I think you're being too hard on yourself."

Darius grunted.

"No, I mean it. You didn't let Indigo down. You've been taking good care of him. It was his idea to escape from the corral, not yours."

"I guess."

"Why don't we head over to the barn and see if he's wandered back there. For all we know, he's already safe and sound inside."

Jax met them halfway up the gravel road to the main museum building. "Did you guys find him?"

"Not yet," Darius said. "But I'm not giving up."

20

Saying It Right

Delta awoke to darkness. After hours of searching in vain for the runaway marsh tacky, Pops had insisted they head home for the night. It had been past midnight by the time she collapsed onto the daybed and immediately fell asleep. As tired as she had been, though, she was surprised to awaken now, in the middle of the night. She blinked toward the clock perched atop a pile of art supply catalogs on Tootsie's desk.

9:43.

Whoa! She had slept through the entire day.

"Morning," Jax yawned from the doorway.

"Huh?"

"I just said, 'Good morning.' Tootsie says we have to get up and start packing. Everybody has to evacuate the island because of the hurricane."

"Is that why it's so dark?" Delta asked. "The hurricane, I mean."

Jax laughed and crossed to the window, where he pulled aside the sheer drapery to reveal a wall of wood. "Pops already latched the shutters closed. He's boarding up the patio door right now."

Delta could hear a distant pounding.

"Tootsie says to pack enough for a few days," Jax told her. "We're going to stay with some friends of theirs in Columbia until the storm passes."

Delta climbed out of bed and rummaged through the top two dresser drawers, which Tootsie had emptied for the summer so Delta wouldn't have to live out of a suitcase. She grabbed shorts, T-shirts, and undies and placed them in the carry-on luggage she had stored in the closet. After brushing her teeth, she repacked her toiletry bag and tossed it in as well.

"Oh, good, sweetie. I see you're all ready to go." Tootsie leaned on her crutches in the hallway. "Your Pops is putting some sandbags around the patio. We should be able to head out in an hour or so."

"Any word on Indigo? Did they find him yet?"

"No, sweetie. Not as far as I know."

Delta sighed as she went out the front door and around the house to where her brother was already helping stack canvas sacks. At the rear of the small yard, a narrow freshwater canal flowed past, its surface choppy in the growing wind.

"Pops, you said that treasure hunter guy should move his cannons or else the tidal surge would get them."

"That's right, Jackson. A storm surge can tear up a beach, wash away dunes, rip out docks. It'd have no problem dragging those relics right back into Port Royal Sound."

Jax's eyes grew wide. "But that giant wave won't wash away your house, will it?"

"No, kiddo, we're a couple of blocks from the ocean. A surge won't do damage this far inland, but hurricanes bring heavy winds and rains. These sandbags will help protect the house in case the canal overflows."

Delta was still thinking of the tidal surge, though. Tearing up the beach. Washing away dunes. "Pops, the turtle nests will be safe, right? I mean, they're buried, so the surge won't get them, will it?"

"Sorry, Delta-boo. I'm afraid there won't be any more turtle boils on the island this year. If the surge doesn't completely wash the nests away, it'll drown the eggs."

"But Tootsie said there are still dozens of nests out there, and each one has like a hundred babies in it," Delta gasped. "They're all going to die now?"

"I know it's sad, sweetie, but it's just nature's way. There's nothing we can do to stop a hurricane." Pops carried one last patio chair around the house toward the garage.

Delta groaned. "If only *we* could have stopped this hurricane, Jax."

He nodded. "We maybe could have prevented it from coming at all if it hadn't been for that stupid *choy-gee-duh* curse."

"What did you just say?"

Jax shrugged. "You know, the Legend of the Three Sisters. *Choy-gee-duh.* Did I say it wrong?"

Delta grabbed her brother in a bear hug. "No, Jax, you said it exactly *right.* You're a genius! You've figured out how to break the turtle's curse!"

"I have?"

Delta nodded. "Hurry up! We've got to stop this storm!"

The siblings pedaled their bikes toward their friend's house at top speed. They had left a note on the kitchen counter explaining that they would *be back soon,* but had offered no other explanation for their sudden disappearance. Tootsie had said they'd be evacuating the island in about an hour, and hopefully this task wouldn't take much longer than that. And anyway, no one would have to evacuate at all if Delta and Jax could stop the storm from coming.

"What in the world are you kids doing over here right now? Are your grandparents okay?" Ruby was shoving suitcases into the trunk of her car. Keisha stood next to her, wearing a pink backpack and carrying an armload of stuffed animals.

"Hi, Uncle D.'s friends. We're going to Aunt Debra's house in Atlanta. Where are you 'vacuating to?"

"Tootsie and Pops have friends in Columbia. We're heading there in about an hour. Is Darius around?"

Ruby shook her head. "He and his dad are still looking for that horse. If they don't find him soon, they're gonna have to hope for the best and meet us in Atlanta. The rest of the family's already left."

She glanced around the yard for one last look. Shutters were closed on all of the houses, glass doors were boarded up, and outdoor furniture and toys were stacked beneath the raised platform that supported the main home. Everything seemed taken care of, except—

"Well, shoot! Micah and C.J. were supposed to bring the boat in."

Delta looked out toward the long dock and could see the johnboat bouncing on the wind-tossed waters of the tidal creek. "We can do it," she offered. "Where do you want it?"

Ruby looked between Delta and Jax, and then at Keisha, who was climbing into her car seat. "You sure, sweeties? I mean, it'd really help me out. I need to get this sugarplum to her mama and daddy."

"No, really. It's no problem," Delta insisted.

Ruby showed them where to place the boat under the house, hugged them both, and then hopped into her car. As she pulled out of the yard, she rolled down the window and shouted a final instruction.

"Once you get that boat put up, y'all get on home. Your grandparents are bound to be worried."

Delta and Jax waved goodbye and headed down the long dock, wind whipping their hair and blowing stray bits of seagrass and Spanish moss into their faces.

The motor started with a tug of the pull-cord. Delta had watched Darius maneuver the little flat-bottomed boat just a couple of days ago, and he had made it seem easy enough. She could see their destination across the marshy waters leading to Port Royal Sound and, shifting the rudder on the engine like Darius had done, was able to steer with no problem. In less than ten minutes, she and her brother had arrived.

"I can't believe we didn't figure this out sooner," she said as they pulled the boat up onto the shore of Chugeeta Island. "I knew *choy-*

ee-gee-doh sounded familiar, but I didn't make the connection until you said it this morning, Jax. This island is named after the sisters, so it must be the right place to break the curse."

"Don't be so hard on yourself. It isn't the *exact* same name. How would you have known?"

Delta shrugged. "I think it *is* the same name, except it got twisted around a bit and mispronounced over the years. Over time, people just forgot what the name originally meant. Darius didn't even know."

"So, now that we're here, where do we bury the turtle?" Jax pulled the amulet from beneath his shirt and lifted the cord from around his neck, allowing the pure white carving to swing in the gusting wind.

Delta reached over and held the little loggerhead in her palm. "Where do you want to go, little turtle? We got you this far, but where do you belong?"

A fallen palmetto frond blew across the kids' feet and down the path through the thick forest.

"That way," Delta said. "To the center of the island."

The branches of the massive live oak at the heart of Chugeeta provided a protective roof over the clearing. Wind whistled through the highest branches, showering thousands of tiny leaves onto the soft, padded ground below. Down here, there was no breeze at all, just a calm August air, scented with earth and plant and warmth. Delta knew the salty waters beyond were roiling as Hurricane Jackson approached, but in this haven, those worries seemed a million miles away. The peacefulness made her feel warm all over, especially in her hand.

My hand? She glanced down in time to see the carved turtle transform into the familiar rosy glow that had already shown her so much. And then the fog.

If experience had taught her anything, Delta knew that she was still standing on Three Sisters Island. Aside from that knowledge, though, everything was different. The hot summer sun beat down on this clearing, which had no shade and no soft, padded floor. Sandy soil, adorned with only a few scattered palmetto shrubs, filled the space, surrounded on all sides by thicker foliage that blocked the waters Delta knew surrounded this islet. The colossal tree that would someday rule Chugeeta was gone and, in its place, a cluster of Native Americans stood with their heads facing the ground.

There was the regal chieftess in her elaborate cape, and there were her triplet daughters. But no. There were only two young women standing with their mother on this day. The remaining villagers circled the family, their solemn expressions a stark contrast to the casual joy Delta had seen in their village just a few days ago. There was no laughter today and no conversation. She searched the crowd for Juan Menéndez, the Spanish governor's son, in his knee-length pants and lace-fronted shirt, but was not surprised that he was nowhere to be seen. He and the third princess were gone forever.

Suddenly the chieftess began to speak in her ancient language. All eyes focused on her as she made sweeping arm movements. Delta wished she could understand this woman's words. A middle-aged man in a loincloth stepped forward and placed a large woven basket at the queen's feet. As she pointed to specific spots on the ground, the man scooped three holes in the sandy soil with a large oyster shell.

The two remaining sisters stepped forward then, and each slowly removed the string of beads she wore around her neck. A carved turtle amulet dangled from each necklace, and Delta watched as one sister, and then the other, silently dropped her precious charm into the newly dug soil. One hole remained empty, and Delta knew now what had happened to that third carved turtle. It had been lost in that long-ago storm on Port Royal Sound by a brave sister attempting to save her friend. It had washed ashore on Hilton Head Island and lay buried in the sand on the beach until a mother loggerhead happened to choose that exact spot to lay her eggs, nearly five hundred years later. Jax had found the carving, and now it was coming home to be with its sisters.

The loinclothed man reached into the basket and handed something to the chieftess, who held up three green saplings for the gathered crowd to see. She placed one young plant into the first sister's hole, atop that princess' amulet, and stepped aside as the man packed dirt around the roots. They repeated the procedure for the second sister's tree, but then stopped when they reached the final, vacant hole.

The queen held the third sapling high. Tears streamed down her face as she spoke loudly and clearly. Delta understood. The grieving mother was saying goodbye to her daughter. The two surviving triplets stood silently, their own tear-streaked faces raised to the sun. The man planted the sapling in the otherwise empty hole as the crowd watched and the clearing filled with fog.

21

Dropping on Down

"Are you kidding me?" Jax faced his sister with his hands on his hips. "You took another trip to the past without me?"

Delta wiped a stray tear from her cheek and allowed her eyes to readjust to the shady dimness of the modern-day islet. "I saw her funeral. It was here on Chugeeta."

Jax's eyes grew wide. "She's buried right here?"

Delta shook her head. "No, I guess her body was lost at sea. But they had a ceremony here. They planted three trees, one for each triplet. The other two sisters buried their turtle amulets with their trees."

"So, the other two carvings are here on this island?"

"Yeah, I mean, assuming no one has moved them, they should be." Delta surveyed her surroundings. "There should be a cluster of three trees about three feet apart. Two of them will have amulets under them, and the third, well, it won't—yet. But if we can figure out which tree belongs to the lost princess, we can bury the carving you found under it."

Jax's face lit up. "And then the three sisters will be reunited. The curse will be broken."

Delta grinned. "That's what the legend says."

Jax retrieved the ancient turtle on its new cord from his sister. "You're nearly home," he told it.

Delta wandered around the edge of the clearing, searching for any group of three trees. The saplings had been small, so she couldn't tell what type they were, but she knew they were not palms. That ruled out about half of the plants on the island. She also assumed they were all the same species, since they represented triplets.

"Finding anything?" Jax called.

"No, not yet. You?"

"Me neither, but I have an idea."

Delta turned to see her brother scaling the trunk of the giant live oak and standing triumphantly in the fern-covered nest in the tree's crotch.

"Jax, quit playing treehouse. We're on a tight schedule here. The storm's coming, and Tootsie and Pops are going to kill us if we're late."

"I'm not playing. I can see everything from up here. I'll find the three sisters' trees."

Delta had scanned the clearing, finding no conspicuous trios of plants, when she heard, "Uh-oh."

"What'd you do now, Jax?"

"No problem. I'll find it."

"Find what, Jax? What did you do?"

"Nothing. I just saw those bushes moving, like some big animal was in there or something. It just startled me is all. I'll find it, though."

Jax was on his hands and knees in the fern nest, digging through the lacy plants. He looked like Darius had when he'd dropped his glasses in Beaufort.

"I found it! It's stuck in a knothole or something."

Delta stopped her search and walked to the base of the tree. "Please tell me you did not almost lose the turtle."

"No biggie. It's right here. It's—"

Through the thick trunk of the tree, Delta couldn't hear what happened next, but Jax could. From his position at the open slit that had been hidden by mossy ferns, he heard the amulet fall through the notch and hit something deep down inside a hollow portion of the tree's massive trunk.

"I'm so sorry, Delta. I'm so, so sorry."

"Jax, where is the turtle?"

"I didn't mean to drop it. I'm so sorry."

Delta sighed. "Well, just pick it up, goofball. It's not that big of a deal. But hurry up. It's starting to rain." Despite the natural roof provided by the live oak's web of branches, fat drops were finding their way to the ground. Out in the open, away from the tree's protection, it was likely raining pretty hard.

"I can't pick it up, Delta. It's gone."

"What do you mean 'gone'?"

Jax slowly descended the tree trunk. When he turned toward his sister, she saw that he was near tears.

"Jax, what happened up there? Did you have another vision or something?"

He shook his head and swallowed hard. "I dropped the amulet, and it fell down a crack in the tree. I tried to get it out, but I think I just knocked it the rest of the way down."

"Down where?"

Jax looked at the ground, unable to meet his sister's gaze. "I guess the trunk is kind of hollow. The turtle sounded like it fell a long way down."

Delta grabbed her brother by the shoulders. "You mean we can't get to it? At all?" Her panic was punctuated by the roar of thunder.

Still staring at the ground, Jax sniffed and shook his head. He spoke so softly that Delta could barely hear him over the intensifying noise of wind gusting through Chugeeta Island's foliage. "I am so sorry."

Delta took a deep breath and sighed. The storm was worsening, the cursed turtle was lost, and they were out of time.

"Come on, Jax. Let's head back. Tootsie and Pops will be crazy worried if we're gone much longer."

"But what about breaking the curse?"

"We've done all we can for now. Maybe Darius can help us figure out a way to get the turtle after the storm passes."

The siblings trudged back up the path to the islet's shore, palmetto shrubs thrashing together in the thick underbrush lining the trail.

"See? That's what startled me," Jax said. "I thought it was a wild animal."

Delta rolled her eyes. "It's probably the wind, Jax. Let's just get in the boat and go home."

A task easier said than done.

22

Braving the Storm

From the open view of the little island's sandy beach, Hurricane Jackson's approach became more ominous. Steady rain pelted the earth as black clouds thickened and white-capped waves covered the waters between Chugeeta and Hilton Head. Delta and Jax fastened their life jackets and dragged the flat-bottomed boat off the beach, jumping into the craft once they were knee-deep in the pounding surf.

The engine started on the second pull of the cord. Delta sat in the rear of the boat, her hand on the motor's steering handle, the taste of salt on her lips as ocean spray stung her cheeks. The rising wind whipped a lock of dripping hair into her face as she watched her brother's slumped shoulders in front of her on the middle seat. She brushed drips from her eyes and told herself they were seawater, not tears.

Squinting through the downpour, Delta strained to see the forested shore of Hilton Head in the distance. Chugeeta had proved an obvious target on their trip out—one tiny islet straight across from Darius' house. But now, from this vantage point, she realized that dozens of similar docks lined the marsh side of Hilton Head. The entire shoreline looked the same from out here on the water. *Which one belongs to the McGees?*

Thunder roared again and Delta frantically scanned the skies, only slightly relieved that no nearby lightning was visible. The danger set in. *We're out on the water in a metal boat during a thunderstorm—a hurricane!* The rain was falling in sheets now, soaking the siblings and completely obscuring the distant docks.

CRRKK!

Delta jumped at the fingernails-on-a-chalkboard sound of metal scraping on something solid. Just to the left of the johnboat, she could see grasses and oyster shells rising above the bouncing waves. Avoiding the oyster beds that filled this waterway had been simple earlier. She had just steered around them on the way to Chugeeta, but now she could barely see ten feet in front of the boat. She jerked on the steering handle until the sound ceased and they had moved again into deeper water.

Just great, she thought, trying not to panic. *If our only choices are getting marooned on a sandbar in the middle of the hurricane or being lost on the deep sea in dying visibility, this is a lose/lose situation.*

The engine made a weird coughing sound, and the boat slowed.

"Why are we stopping, Delta?"

"We're not," she shouted over the storm as the motor sputtered and died. "I mean, not on purpose anyway." She pulled the starter cord once, twice, three times with no results. *"No, no, no! This can't be happening!"*

She yanked the cord again and again, but the engine was done. The little boat bounced on the whitecaps, no longer moving toward Hilton Head. Carried by the tidal stream, it would float out to Port Royal Sound and on into the open Atlantic Ocean. Delta recalled watching Juan Menéndez and his princess paddle to their own end in just such a storm.

"I've really screwed up, Jax. I should never have suggested we come out here in this weather and especially not by ourselves. I don't have a clue what I'm doing." Delta's tears blended with the rain running down her cheeks. *"I'm so stupid!"*

Jax twisted in his seat to face his sister. "No you're not, Delta. I always know I can count on you, but even you can't do *everything* right. Nobody's perfect. I mean, I mess up *all* the time, but I don't think that makes me a bad person. Do you?"

Delta sniffled. "Of course not. You're a great person, Jax."

"Thanks!"

Delta managed a small smile. "But you do mess up a lot."

The siblings both chuckled.

"Yeah, but do you know why I make so many mistakes, Delta? Pops says it's because I'm not afraid to fail sometimes. I always want to do my best, but I don't worry so much about screwing up because I figure I'll do better next time. Pops says that's how you learn stuff—by taking chances."

Delta had never thought of it that way. Her goofy brother's impulsivity often got him into trouble, but he never seemed to let his blunders get him down. He kept trying new things and truly seemed to like himself no matter what.

"You know what, buddy? You're one of the bravest people I know."

"So, I'm your hero?" Jax said with a grin.

"Sure," she replied with a roll of her eyes. "You're my hero."

Two girls laughed then—Delta and another.

"It's her! It's the Marsh Maiden," Jax shouted, pointing to a dark-haired girl in a wooden canoe just feet in front of the johnboat.

His sister shifted in her seat to see the ghost of the third triplet—the tribal princess who had sacrificed her own life trying to save Pedro Menéndez's lost son from a storm so many years ago. Even in the driving rain, her buckskin dress and long silky hair seemed dry, and her black eyes sparkled as she smiled kindly at the stranded siblings.

As Delta moved, though, her foot hit something hard hidden beneath a tarp on the bottom of the boat.

"Oars, Jax! I found a pair of oars!"

Under the watchful eye of the Marsh Maiden, Delta joined her brother on the middle bench seat and the kids maneuvered the aluminum shafts into place, inserting the metal pins into the corresponding holes on the wall of the boat. They had spent much of this summer paddling Pops' kayak, so, although different, rowing wasn't completely foreign to them. After a few mistimed splashes, they synchronized their rowing and moved forward through the choppy waves.

The Marsh Maiden had waited patiently while the duo initially struggled with the oars, but now she paddled slowly ahead of them, always within view, guiding them. Unlike the siblings, who sat in their boat as they followed her, the princess knelt on one knee as she smoothly stroked her paddle through the roiling waters, unfazed by the storm. Delta supposed a ghost had no reason to be afraid of a hurricane, but still. The Native American girl hadn't *always* been a ghost but had apparently always been brave.

"You know, Jax, I've been thinking lately—Juan Menéndez and the Marsh Maiden were willing to risk their actual lives for their people."

"Yeah, so?"

"Well, I was thinking that if they could do something as brave as that, us sacrificing familiar surroundings for Mom and Dad isn't such a big deal. You know?"

Jax nodded. "I guess so, but I still wish we didn't have to move to Siberia."

"Yeah."

Delta and Jax dragged their oars through the powerful tide, happy that at least they were no longer worried about finding their way. As the minutes passed, Delta realized that rowing in the maiden's wake had become easier, the waters around her calmer than the surrounding seas. Magically calmer.

Before long, Delta could see the end of a dock through the pouring rain and, rising above the shore behind it, Darius' stilted house.

"We made it!" Jax shouted.

The Marsh Maiden laughed playfully and, with a friendly smile, nodded a goodbye to the duo in the flat-bottomed boat. Turning her canoe back toward open water, she disappeared into the coming storm as if into a cloak of fog.

23

Awaiting the Worst

Delta and Jax floated the johnboat to shore, walking along the long dock as they towed the boat by its rope. Once back on solid ground, they retrieved the wheeled cart from beneath the house and used it to roll the boat into that sheltered space where the family had secured other outdoor items. Jax insisted on taking charge of tying the boat securely to a large post, using a complex knot he had learned at Boy Scout camp. Then the siblings climbed on their bikes for the wet ride home to face their grandparents.

"I'm glad we made it back alive," Jax said, "but Tootsie and Pops are going to kill us."

"You think so?"

"Um, yeah. Pretty sure."

Delta followed her brother's gaze to the end of Darius' driveway. Parked near the street, its windshield wipers still sweeping from side to side, sat Pops' pickup truck. In front of it, illuminated by two shining headlights, stood the man himself, arms crossed over his chest and rain cascading over the rim of his baseball cap like a waterfall.

"What in the sweet blue blazes were you kids thinking? Get your keisters in this truck *now*."

"But what about our bikes, Pops?"

"I said *now!*"

Delta and Jax climbed into the pickup without another word, dripping rainwater all over the leather seats. A couple of loud bangs indicated the moments Pops tossed their bicycles into the truck bed, and then he climbed into the driver's seat and slammed his door shut. With both hands gripping the steering wheel, he turned to face his grandkids.

"You know, your grandmother is a nervous wreck. I've been driving all over our neighborhood looking for you. Of course, it never entered our minds that you'd have come all the way over *here* just as we're getting ready to evacuate."

"Then how'd you find us?" Jax asked. Delta elbowed him and gave him a wide-eyed stare.

"I probably *wouldn't* have found you, but Ruby called to make sure you got home alright."

Oh, yeah. Miss Ruby.

"She said you were going to move the johnboat and then get right on home, but you sure must've taken your sweet time about it. You've been gone for hours. We were worried sick."

So, Pops didn't actually see us in the boat, Delta thought, relieved. *He must have gotten to Darius' house while we were putting it under the house.*

He shook his head and inserted the key into the ignition. "I admire you wanting to come check on your friends, but don't ever scare us like that again, you hear?"

"Yes, sir."

"We won't."

The trio rode in silence toward home, having to turn around and take an alternate route at one point when they encountered a fallen tree in the road. The rain was still falling in sheets, appearing in some places to be coming down sideways. The windshield wipers swiped at full speed, trying in vain to clear water and the occasional flying palmetto frond.

"We're sorry we scared you and Tootsie, Pops. We thought we'd be back home before you guys were ready to evacuate."

"Well, Delta, that won't be an issue now. A truck pulling a flatbed trailer had an accident on the bridge, and they've had to close it."

"Close the bridge? But then how will we go to Columbia?"

"We won't, Jackson. We'll be sticking out the storm here."

Delta and Jax stared at each other. Because of them, the family wouldn't be able to evacuate the island. Rather than safely visiting with their grandparents' friends in the state capital, they'd be spending the night barricaded in a shuttered house while Hurricane Jackson raged right outside. *Man, we really did it this time. No wonder Pops is so mad,* Delta thought.

Even harder to take, though, was Tootsie's reaction when they walked into the house.

"Oh my goodness, you're both *alright!*" Tossing her crutches aside, Tootsie hobbled toward the door and grabbed first Delta and then Jax in a bear hug. Tears streamed down her cheeks as she examined them both for injuries.

"Are you hurt? What happened? We were so worried, we just didn't know what to do!"

Delta felt awful. She had made her own grandmother cry, and all for nothing, because they had lost the amulet and now the turtle's curse was completely—and literally—out of their hands.

"We're so sorry, Tootsie. We didn't expect to be gone so long, and we didn't know the bridge was going to close."

"Yeah, we didn't mean to cause so much trouble," Jax added.

Tootsie wiped her eyes and smiled. "Well, I'm just so happy you're both okay. Just having us all together makes me feel *worlds* better."

Pops brought in a stack of towels from the bathroom, and he and the kids dried themselves enough to at least stop dripping all over the floor. Then they each retreated to their rooms to change into fresh clothes.

Even though it was still late afternoon, the house had an eerie feeling of nighttime since the shutters were all latched closed. Wind howled outside, and rain pounded on the roof overhead. The TV was on in the living room so, for lack of anything else to do, the family clustered around it watching the latest weather reports. Judy Drench seemed delighted with the arrival of Hurricane Jackson, grinning broadly as she shouted an update from the beach while surfers tackled the enormous waves behind her.

"Just look at that. You'd have to be truly devoted to your sport to take a surfboard out in weather like this," Tootsie said.

"Or a bit nuts," Pops chimed in. "Can you imagine the kind of person crazy enough to purposely go out in the ocean during a hurricane?"

Delta and Jax shared a glance but said nothing. They'd been lucky to make it back from Chugeeta this afternoon. In fact, if the Marsh Maiden hadn't come to rescue them when she did, they probably wouldn't be sitting here in their grandparents' living room watching television right now. Maybe she hadn't been able to save Juan Menéndez, but Delta was sure glad the princess had stuck around to save her and Jax.

POP! POP! POP!

Thunder boomed outside as Tootsie pulled a bag of popcorn from the microwave. Weather reports droned on in the background as the family played board games to pass the time. With the house sealed up from the storm and the electricity still working—for now, at least— the grandparents strived to make the atmosphere more cozy than frightening. Even so, when bedtime came, Jax insisted on sleeping on the floor in Delta's room "just in case she got scared of sleeping alone."

"How bad is the hurricane going to be, Pops?" Jax asked when their grandfather stopped by to say good night.

"We won't know that until morning, kiddo. In the meantime, sweet dreams."

Delta lay awake for hours, though, hearing the storm rage. How could she have sweet dreams when her world was such a nightmare?

24

Reaching a Compromise

Delta awoke the next morning to sunlight streaming through her bedroom window. For a moment, that seemed perfectly natural. Then, remembering the darkness of the hurricane, she wondered if she had just dreamed the whole storm/Siberia/curse thing. But then she saw Jax wrapped in a blanket on her floor and realized that all of it had been much too real.

"Jax, wake up."

He grunted and pulled the covers tighter.

"Jax! It's morning, and I think the storm is over."

"Rise and shine, sleepyheads!" Tootsie stood cheerfully in the doorway. "Pops has already opened the shutters and is taking the plywood off the patio door. I've got breakfast ready if you're hungry."

Suddenly, Delta was starving. Although Pops had stuck a frozen pizza in the oven last night, she'd been too unsettled to eat much. Now, this morning, her stomach clamored for food. Following Tootsie into the kitchen, though, Delta noticed something strange.

"Hey! Where are your crutches?"

Still wearing her black cast boot, Tootsie was barely even limping. "My ankle feels a lot better today, and those crutches just made my armpits hurt."

The smell of bacon had finally roused Jax from sleep, and he joined them at the table. Suddenly, natural light filled the room as Pops removed the boards anchored to the outside of the sliding glass door. Seeing the rest of the family at the table, he smiled and waved. Tootsie slid the door open and invited him to join them.

"Now that's an offer I can't refuse. I haven't had much appetite the past few days because of that cold I had, but right now I believe I could eat a horse!"

Delta stopped chewing, a forkful of pancakes midway to her mouth. This was all so weird. Everybody cheerful and healthy, with the sun shining and all. *What's going on?*

"So how bad was the storm, Pops?" Jax asked.

"Well, turns out Hurricane Jackson was all bark and no bite. The news this morning said he petered out overnight and headed out to the open ocean. You can never really predict what a storm like that will do, but I swear I've never seen anything make such a drastic change as this one did, and so suddenly."

"Is there any damage to the house, dear?"

Pops shook his head and took a sip of coffee. "None at all. I mean there are some small branches and leaves down in the yard, but they'll be easy to clean up."

"We'll help, Pops!"

"Why thank you, Delta-boo. I'd appreciate that. From what I can see, none of the neighbors have any real damage, either. I'd say we really dodged a bullet this time."

The wall phone rang then, and Pops rose to answer it. After a brief greeting, he stretched the coiled cord around the corner into the living room to continue his conversation.

Delta gulped orange juice and then had another thought. *What about the turtle nests? Did the storm surge drown the baby turtles?*

Tootsie clapped her hands together. "Oh, I didn't tell you yet. I spoke to my friend Geneva from the Turtle Team earlier. Apparently, there was no tidal surge at all, so all of the remaining nests appear to be unharmed."

"So, they'll all hatch now?" Jax asked.

Tootsie nodded. "As long as that Nest Vandal leaves them alone, the hatchlings should do just fine."

Pops walked back into the kitchen, holding the telephone in his outstretched hand. "It's your folks, kiddos. Making sure we're all A-OK."

Jax got to the phone first this time and grabbed the receiver, Delta placing her head close to his so they could both hear their parents. "Hey, we lived through a hurricane!"

"We know, Jax!" Dad said. "And we're so glad you did!"

"It was kind of scary, though. I mean, Delta was scared—"

"I was not! . . . Well, maybe a little."

Mom laughed. "I bet you were both very brave and a big help to Tootsie and Pops."

Delta glanced at her brother. Pops clearly hadn't told their parents about their "missing persons" escapade yesterday.

"Listen, kids. We wanted to talk to you about something else, too." Dad sounded serious. *Oh no. That again.* With the successful morning they'd had so far, Delta had nearly managed to forget her family was moving across the world in a couple of weeks.

"Yeah, we're listening," she said.

She heard Dad take a deep breath before speaking. "You guys know how important you are to us, right? How much we love you?"

"Well, sure." Jax and Delta raised their eyebrows at each other. It wasn't like Dad to get all mushy.

"Our family is top priority, but part of being a parent is making sure you show your kids the importance of setting goals and achieving them. For example, professional goals."

"We get it, Dad. We already had this conversation, and Jax and I agreed that you and Mom should take the jobs in Siberia. We know how important this opportunity is to your careers."

"And we're really proud of you," Jax added.

That sounded strange to Delta, but it was true. Her parents often said they were proud of her and her brother's accomplishments—grades, Scout achievements, sports victories, and such. But she couldn't ever remember bothering to say the same to them.

"Yeah, we really are," she said.

"Aw, sweeties, you're the best," Mom replied, listening in on speakerphone. "But Tootsie and Pops have come up with a compromise of sorts, and we wanted to get your thoughts on it."

Delta glanced over her shoulder at her grandparents, both watching expectantly from the kitchen table.

"What would you guys think," Dad began, "if the two of you lived with Tootsie and Pops for the year while we're on this expedition? We'll come home for a few weeks during your winter break, and we'll call every chance we get."

"Live on Hilton Head, for real?"

"That's right, Jax."

"And we'd go to school here?"

"Yep. School, Scouts, sports. Whatever you want. Tootsie and Pops have invited you to stay and make *their* home *your* home."

Delta's heart leaped. After a summer on the Carolina island, Hilton Head already felt like home to her. She would miss her parents, sure, but she had been away from them this summer. With her grandparents there, life had been just fine. Better than fine, now that their luck seemed to have turned. She couldn't speak for her brother, but Delta thought this was a grand idea!

"*Woohoo!*" Jax shouted and then reined in his enthusiasm. "No offense, Mom and Dad. We love you guys, too, but we were really going to miss America."

Dad chuckled.

"No offense taken, kiddo. I know this won't be the same as staying in Chicago, but you'll have familiar surroundings, at least, and you'll be in good hands with Tootsie and Pops."

"We'll be in great hands," Delta said.

"We're going to live with you!" Jax shouted, running to the table and throwing his arms around Pops' shoulders.

"We promise to be on our best behavior the whole time we're here," Delta told her parents.

After all, what kind of trouble could a couple of good kids get into?

By lunchtime, Delta and Jax had helped Pops clear the windblown sticks and fallen leaves from the yard. Several bags of lawn waste now sat by the street, ready for pickup. The kids dragged the last of the heavy sandbags around to the side of the garage from the patio, then headed into the house to wash up.

Munching on a tuna sandwich, Delta swallowed and turned to her grandfather.

"Um, Pops. Jax and I want to apologize again for taking off yesterday without talking to you first." With his mouth full across the table, Jax nodded his agreement.

Pops narrowed his eyes. "I know you're sorry, but what's most important is that you both realize now what a dangerous thing you did, heading out into the storm like that."

"Oh, believe me, we know," Jax said. The siblings shared a look as Pops smiled at his grandkids.

"I know we were supposed to evacuate the island, but I've got to admit I'm glad we're not battling all the traffic trying to get back today. Seeing as how you've learned your lesson and been such a big help this morning, I'd say all is forgiven. Now, what would you like to do this afternoon?"

Delta swallowed hard, realizing the irony of her request. "Um, Pops, would it be okay if we rode our bikes over to Darius' house?"

25

Confessing the Truth

Mac waved from atop a tall extension ladder, where he was opening up the storm shutters on his stilted house. Darius rolled a wheelbarrow, loaded with fallen branches, around the side of the building, dropping the handles so that the braces of the barrow hit the ground with a thud. Several smaller sticks bounced out into the yard, but Darius ignored them and heaved a sigh.

"Hey! Y'all survived your first hurricane!"

Jax dropped his bike in the grass and ran toward his friend. "Hey, guess what? We're moving to Hilton Head."

Darius shrugged. "You already live on Hilton Head."

"No, we're *moving* here, like for the whole year."

The corner of Darius' mouth lifted slightly but not enough for Delta to consider it an actual smile.

"Really?"

Delta propped her bicycle carefully on its kickstand and joined the boys. "Tootsie and Pops invited us to live with them while Mom and Dad do their work in Siberia. We'll go to school here and everything."

"Won't you miss your parents?" Darius asked.

"Well, sure," Delta said. "But we can talk to them on the phone, and they're going to come visit sometimes."

"Yeah, it's not like the days of Santa Elena, Darius," Jax chimed in. "We won't be the *lost kids* our parents have to search for."

Delta chuckled. "True, and anyway, we'll be with Tootsie and Pops. It'll be just like this summer, except during the school year."

"Sweet. I'm happy for y'all." Darius didn't sound happy, though, and he definitely didn't look happy.

"Are you okay?" Delta asked.

"There's still no sign of Indigo. He's been gone for almost two days now, and we've looked *everywhere*."

Mac climbed down the ladder and walked over to the kids, placing an arm around his son's shoulders. "The sheriff's department is on the lookout for him. They'll let us know if someone reports a sighting. Maybe a family will return from evacuating and find him standing in their carport or something. Wouldn't that be a welcome-home surprise?"

Mac laughed, clearly trying to raise Darius' spirits. "In any case, it wasn't your fault, D. Indy's always had an independent streak. Why don't you just take a break and visit with your friends for a bit?"

Darius nodded glumly, and the trio headed back to the fire pit, taking seats in the still-damp wooden Adirondack chairs.

"Hey, Darius, guess what else? I lost the turtle amulet, and it didn't even matter. The bad stuff all got fixed even without breaking the curse."

Delta shot her brother a stern look. *All* the bad stuff hadn't been fixed. "I bet Indy turns up now that the weather is clear again."

Darius looked up at Jax. "What do you mean *lost* the amulet? Where did you lose it?"

"On Chugeeta. Did you know that ginormous tree has a hollow space in its trunk? I dropped the turtle down in there by accident."

"What are you talking about, Jax? That didn't happen. I took y'all over there days ago, and I've seen you with the amulet since then."

Delta glanced sheepishly at her friend. "We figured out that 'Chugeeta' sounds a lot like the Native American word your dad used for 'three sisters'—*choy-ee-gee-doh*."

"Huh. I guess it does, kinda. So?"

"So, that sounded like where the amulet might belong, don't you think? And we'd been trying to figure out all along where it belongs, right?"

"Yeah," Darius agreed.

Delta took a deep breath. "Please don't be mad, Darius, but we borrowed your boat yesterday and took it to Chugeeta Island."

"You *what*? Yesterday? Just the two of you?"

"It was while you were out looking for your horse."

"Are you kidding me, Jax? I mean, I wouldn't mind loaning y'all my boat sometime if I thought you *knew how to use it*. And if it wasn't during a *hurricane*!"

Delta kept her eyes to the ground. "We know. It was crazy. We should never have done it."

Darius shook his head and stared at the bright blue sky for a moment before looking back at Jax. "So, wait. You dropped the turtle down *inside* the tree?"

"Yeah. I was up in the nest, and it fell into a crack under the ferns. When I tried to yank it out, it fell down inside where I couldn't reach."

"Huh. I didn't know it was hollow."

"Me, neither, but I guess it is. Partly, anyway."

Darius was thoughtful for a moment. "How big is the opening?"

Jax placed his forefingers and thumbs together to indicate the size.

"Did you still have it on that leather cord?"

Jax nodded.

"I might be able to hook it if we take a fishing rod over there," Darius said. "We'd need a light to see down into the hole, though."

Jax reached into the pocket of his cargo shorts and pulled out his red-tinted flashlight. "Ta-da! I put colored cellophane over the lens for the turtle boil, so the hatchlings wouldn't get confused and think my light was the moon, but that's a quick fix." He removed the rubber band holding the transparent red plastic in place and then poked the button to produce a bright white light. "See?"

"Excellent! Dad and I already moved the boat back to the dock, so we should be good to go."

Delta chewed on her lip.

"Um, Darius. There's something else we haven't told you. It's about your boat."

"What about it?"

"The motor died on our way back from Chugeeta yesterday."

Darius laughed. "Oh, that! It's an old motor. It's just kind of touchy sometimes."

"But I think I really broke it somehow, Darius. I mean, I couldn't get it started again, and I yanked on the cord a bunch of times."

"Well, you must have started it eventually, or you wouldn't be sitting here right now."

Jax shook his head. "We rowed back. We found oars under a tarp in the boat."

Darius' brow furrowed. "The two of you rowed all the way back in the storm?"

"That's the best part, Darius," Jax said. "It wasn't just the two of us. The Marsh Maiden showed up in her canoe and led us right back to your dock."

Delta nodded vigorously. "He's telling the truth. It was raining so hard we could barely see where we were going. And, anyway, all the docks look the same from out there. We didn't know what to do at first when the engine died, but then we heard the girl laughing and found the oars. She stayed right in front of us all the way to your house."

Darius looked back and forth between his two friends.

"I know you think we're just making this up, but we're really not," Delta said. "I *swear* it happened just like we said. The Marsh Maiden rescued us."

After a moment of silence, Darius spoke. "I do believe you, and for two reasons. One, I've seen that girl myself a couple of times. Remember, I figured out that the princess we saw in our vision on the beach turned out to be the Marsh Maiden?"

"That's right. And what's the second reason?"

Darius raised a pair of fingers. "Number two, it is actually easier to believe that you were saved by a legendary ghost princess than it is to imagine the two of you dumbbells in a hurricane rowing your way to my dock all by yourselves!"

26

Finding the Three

Sunlight danced across the waters leading out to Chugeeta Island as the little johnboat sliced through the smooth, flat surface. Fortunately, Darius had been able to start the engine with no problem after fiddling with its wires and tubes a bit. He easily maneuvered through a maze of sandbars, their marsh grasses swaying lazily in the calm breeze. A great blue heron stared at them from atop a bed of black and white oysters, and a flock of pelicans floated calmly overhead. Delta recalled her last trip across this waterway and felt like she was in an entirely different place.

"It's amazing how everything just went back to normal. It's like the storm never happened."

"This time it did," Darius said. "But if Hurricane Jackson had been as bad as they predicted, the island might have been recovering for months. No electricity or fresh water, damaged houses and roads, boats wrecked, chunks of beach washed away. The last big hurricane left so many downed trees, it took nearly a year to haul all of them away. We were really lucky this time."

Delta agreed they were lucky about the storm and about all the other things that were better today than yesterday. In fact, Darius' still-missing horse was about the only dark spot in this otherwise sunny day.

The trio pulled the boat to shore on Chugeeta, where gentle waves lapped against the sandy beach. Other than the occasional piece of driftwood washed onto the islet, there was no obvious evidence of yesterday's savage weather.

"Let's do some turtle fishing," Darius said as he toted a rod and reel up the heavily wooded path to the magnificent live oak tree.

Emerging from the trail, though, all three kids stopped in their tracks. Their mouths hung open as great patches of sunlight glared into the clearing at the middle of the little island. The giant tree trunk, with its fern-carpeted nest, was no more.

"How could this happen?"

Delta's breath caught in her throat. Just twenty-four hours ago, she had stood right here protected by the umbrella of the tree's never-ending branches. Jax had towered above her in the aerie where those branches diverged—a spot she had imagined a few days ago as being the center of everything. But now that spot was gone.

"I think lightning might have hit it." Darius had climbed over a portion of the fallen tree to reach its core. "See, there's charred wood there in the middle."

The afternoon sun beat down in patches that, just yesterday, had been fully shaded by the thick foliage above. Delta and Jax carefully traversed what had been a field of fallen leaves but was now a forest of leaning branches. Pushing aside a hanging clump of Spanish moss, the siblings ducked beneath an arched tree limb and gasped.

"Geez! It looks like it exploded," Jax said.

The colossal trunk that had supported the live oak for hundreds of years had split apart like the peel of a banana. Three separate sections, each as big around as a patio table, lay splayed in different directions, their roots now perpendicular to the ground. The acrid smell of smoke rose from the burned base of each fallen remnant.

"It looks like lightning hit the center and just blew it apart," Darius said.

Tears stung Delta's eyes. This oak had been the very heart of Chugeeta Island for generations. Sitting up high in that tree, on a cushion of feathery ferns, she had felt safe from all the worries of the outside world.

Jax scaled one of the tumbled trunk sections and peered over its top into the crater left by its downfall. "No way! You guys are never gonna believe what I found!"

Darius and Delta climbed up the base of the tree to where Jax dangled into the hole beneath, Delta instinctively grabbing the back of her brother's shirt to prevent his own fall. Below them, shallow roots protruded from the base of each overturned bole.

"I'd have expected the roots to be a lot longer, Darius. You know, to go deeper into the ground."

"Some kinds of trees have roots like that, Delta, but not live oaks. Most of theirs grow sideways instead of deep."

Jax had pulled free of his sister's grasp and descended into the hole, clinging to roots like ladder rungs. He dropped the last several feet and squatted onto the newly exposed sandy soil. "Woohoo! Just look what I found!"

A thought struck Delta. *Maybe something good has come from the oak's destruction.* "Is it the amulet? Did it fall all the way to the bottom?"

"You bet it did! And guess what was waiting for it?" Jax leaned back so that Delta and Darius could see the treasures he had found. Delta laughed out loud while Darius just looked confused.

"Am I seeing triple?" he asked. Three nearly identical carved loggerhead turtles lay at the bottom of the crater along with an assortment of tiny beads and the charred remnants of a leather cord. "What the—"

"Oh, yeah," Delta laughed. "I guess there was one more thing we forgot to tell you."

"Well, what do you know?" Darius said.

After everything he had learned and experienced since meeting the Wells kids, Delta's final vision was the piece that completed the mysterious puzzle they'd been working to solve all week. Here on Chugeeta Island nearly five hundred years ago, the two surviving princesses had buried their precious amulets beneath baby trees, along with an extra sapling to represent their lost sister. Now, thanks to Delta and Jax and a well-aimed bolt of lightning, the three matching turtle carvings had finally been reunited.

"Warn us if one of them starts turning red," Darius called down to Jax, who was still stooped over the reunited amulets. But all three turtles remained a cool pearly white.

Delta shook her head. "I don't think Jax's turtle is going to send us on any more trips through time. The carving showed us the hints we needed to help find its sisters, and now it's back where it truly belongs."

Jax nodded from the bottom of the hole, where he was inspecting the exposed roots. His eyes grew wide as he shouted, "No wonder we couldn't find a triangle of trees, Delta. The three saplings grew together into one gigantic live oak."

The kids examined the three fallen sections, seeing that each did indeed have its own distinct root system. The massive trunk had actually been three separate trees bound together through time. "This tree *is* the three sisters, guys. They had wanted to be together all along, but now that the amulets are all in one place—"

Delta grinned. "You're right, Jax. We really *did* break the turtle's curse!"

The sound of crackling timber interrupted their celebration.

"Whoa! What was that, y'all?" Darius and Delta clung to the edge of the root ball as nearby branches shifted, scattering leaves to the ground.

Still at the base of the crater, Jax called up to them. "What's going on? What was that noise?"

Limbs of the fallen trees thrashed as something large passed by on the ground below.

"Darius, are there any wild animals out here on Chugeeta?" Delta asked, her voice shaking.

"Sure, little ones, I guess. Raccoons and birds and stuff." A loud crash signaled a creature sneaking ever closer through the newfound denseness of this previously cleared area of the island. "But nothing that big!"

The two older kids both jumped over the rim of the trunk and clung to roots on the interior of the hole.

"I told you there was a wild animal out here," Jax shouted. "You didn't believe me, Delta, but I told you."

Delta ducked beneath the top of the tree trunk. "Can you see anything, Darius?"

Peeking over the edge, he spied a large black shape passing through the storm debris. A thick branch shuddered and gave way as the beast forced its way through the foliage. Darius gasped. "It can't be!"

"What?" Jax cried from below. "What can't it be?"

"Indy! How did *you* get here?" The marsh tacky twitched his ears and whinnied happily at the sound of Darius' voice. Aside from some leaves and sticks clinging to his coat, he looked just fine. Delta and Darius scrambled over the edge and down the fallen tree trunk, with Jax not far behind.

"You have no idea how happy I am to see you, boy." Darius stroked Indy's mane and allowed the horse to nuzzle his neck. Delta couldn't decide which of the two looked happier.

"How *do* you suppose he got to Chugeeta, Darius?" she asked.

"He must have swum over. Marsh tackies are strong swimmers, but I wouldn't have expected him to come *this* far."

Delta recalled the trio's vision on the beach at Hilton Head. They had seen marsh tackies falling from the sinking Spanish galleon into Port Royal Sound. If Indy could make it to Chugeeta, hopefully some of those horses made it safely to shore, too.

"You know, I told you we used to board him and Honey over on Daufuskie Island. Maybe he thought he was going back there."

"Did he used to swim to Daufuskie?"

Hugging his horse around the neck, Darius laughed. "Of course not, Jax. We took them over on the ferry. But all the weird weather must have spooked him; he just wanted to get back to someplace familiar as fast as he could."

"I'll bet he was surprised when he got here and realized it wasn't his old home then," Jax said.

Delta brushed leaves off the tacky's rump. "Maybe, but he was probably just glad to finally be on land. At least he made it here before the hurricane."

"How can you be sure?" Darius asked.

"Because we heard him in the bushes yesterday, except we didn't know it was him," Jax replied. "Admit it, Delta. I was right about there being a big wild animal loose on the island, wasn't I?"

"Oh, Indy's wild, for sure. A vicious, ferocious beast!"

The kids all laughed, and Indigo joined in with a loud neigh and a toss of his head. Then Darius grew serious. "There's just one problem, y'all. How're we going to get him back to Hilton Head?"

27

Nabbing the Culprit

After much discussion, the kids grabbed a rope from the boat and tied the marsh tacky to a tree on the shore of Chugeeta Island while they went back home and told Mac the news. Within an hour, Darius' dad had borrowed a neighbor's pontoon boat and ferried Indigo safely back to the Island History Museum. Honeybee was delighted to have her mate rejoin her in the pasture.

Deciding that touching sacred relics could have less than favorable consequences, the trio had also agreed to leave the three turtle amulets where they'd found them, in the crater that once held the three sisters' trees. Mac and Pops were thrilled when the kids told them about the discovery, though, and the kids were more than happy to pass that responsibility on to the adults.

Mom and Dad arrived on the island a few days later to visit with the kids before heading off on their meteorite hunt. Everyone traded enthusiastic hugs as they met at the airport curb, but Delta's brow furrowed when she noticed the several large suitcases her parents had brought along.

"I thought you said the Field Museum in Chicago was shipping your gear overseas."

"They are," Dad replied. "This stuff is all for you."

Delta and Jax exchanged a nervous glance. Had the plans changed? Were they going to have to move to Siberia after all?

Sensing their confusion, though, Mom spoke up. "We want Hilton Head to seem as much like home for you kiddos as possible while we're gone, so we've brought all your favorite things—clothes, books, posters, video games. The works!"

Tootsie smiled. "Don't worry, dear. We'll make sure they feel at home."

Delta grinned. They already did.

Having anticipated the need for extra space, Tootsie and Pops had both driven to the airport. After the family loaded suitcases into the back of Pops' truck, Jax and Dad slid onto the front bench seat.

"See you in a few minutes," Dad called with a wave as the truck pulled from the curb.

Happy to have a semiprivate moment, Delta hugged her mother's arm as they followed Tootsie toward her car in the parking lot.

"Mom, sometime while you and Dad are here, do you think you could tell me more about your ancestors who came here from Cuba?"

"Well, sure, honey. What do you want to know?"

"Oh, just everything," Delta said. "Like, who they were and when they came here and how. Like, did you know they probably came to Cuba from Spain?"

Mom smiled. "Yes, I guess I did know that, but we've never talked about it much. To be honest, Delta, you and Jax never seemed especially interested in learning about your heritage."

Delta squeezed her mother's arm tighter. "Well, I'm interested now. I figure it's about time I learned something about my people. I mean, how is anyone going to remember them unless we tell their stories?"

At Pops' suggestion, the group headed to the Geechee Grill to sample some great Gullah cooking. Sitting on the restaurant's outdoor patio, Delta and Jax sipped sweet tea beneath a striped umbrella as they awaited the delicious food that Miss Ruby was undoubtedly preparing in the Grill's kitchen.

"Well, if it isn't my favorite family!" Mac approached the table, arms spread wide.

"How's it going, my friend?" Pops asked.

"Just great. I've got the exhibit up and running at the Santa Elena Museum. You'll have to come by and see the finished product."

"We'll definitely do that," Pops said.

"Oh, and you kids might be interested to know I spoke to the Tribal Council about the amulets. We agree that the best place for those three turtles is right where their original owners wanted them to be—in the ground on Three Sisters Island." He chuckled and shook his head. "I still can't believe I never made the connection between *Tso'i igido* and Chugeeta. The three sisters were practically in my backyard all these years, and I didn't even know it."

Darius arrived then in his restaurant uniform and bright red oven mitts, hefting a large stainless-steel pot. "Hope y'all are hungry," he said.

Delta and Jax gasped as the shiny silver pot began to tip and then flipped over entirely. Steaming piles of shrimp, sausage, potatoes, and corn on the cob poured across the paper tablecloth.

"Way to go, Darius."

"Stop it, Jax. It's okay, Darius. We can clean this up." Delta grabbed napkins from a bucket in the middle of the table but realized the adults were all just grinning at her.

"What?"

"Haven't y'all ever seen a Lowcountry boil?" Darius said, laughing.

"Huh?"

Mac patted Delta on the shoulder. "A Lowcountry boil is like a New England clambake. It's supposed to be served like this. You just eat it right off the table with your fingers."

"You're kidding, right?"

Pops laughed. "He's dead serious, Delta-boo. Just another one of the joys of Sea Island life."

She glanced around the table and saw her parents peeling shrimp and biting into buttery corn with gusto. Even Tootsie was using her hands to nab a chunk of smoked sausage.

"Whatever then," Jax said with a shrug, grabbing a small red potato. "It smells great."

Delta hesitantly joined their messy—but tasty—fun. With juice running down her arms, she appreciated when Darius delivered a couple of rolls of paper towels to the table.

"Hey, y'all. It's that treasure hunter guy."

Across the patio, in the shade of a purple crepe myrtle, Jack Strader and another man were sitting at a table eating fried chicken and waffles.

Pops wiped his mouth with a wad of paper towel and took a gulp of tea. "You know, I read in the paper that he was the cause of the bridge closing before the hurricane."

"How'd he close the bridge, Pops?"

"His truck did it, Jackson. He was hauling those cannons of his on the back of a flatbed truck but apparently didn't have them fastened down properly. Halfway up, the cannons started rolling off and blocked the whole bridge to the mainland."

"Really?"

"Yep. I heard a couple of them went right over the edge into the Intracoastal Waterway."

"Serves him right," Jax said. "I think he was the one messing with all the turtle nests on the beach. We heard him say he'd be glad when they were gone."

As if on cue, a sheriff's car with flashing red lights pulled to a stop in the nearby parking lot, closely followed by the Channel 1 News van. A tall man with curly black hair jumped out of the van holding a microphone and positioned himself not far beyond the waist-high brick wall bordering the restaurant's patio. A young woman with a video camera accompanied him.

"This is Harrison Smalls with a special report for Channel 1 News."

"I guess Judy Drench got bored with Hilton Head once the storm fizzled out," Delta said, rolling her eyes.

"The Beaufort County Sheriff's Department has announced that they have identified the person who has destroyed several Hilton Head Island nesting sites of the endangered loggerhead sea turtle in recent weeks. This illegal activity, committed by the so-called Nest Vandal, was documented heavily by our own Channel 1 News team in the days leading up to Hurricane Jackson."

"Wow! They're going to arrest him, and we're getting a front-row seat," Jax said, looking toward the treasure hunter.

Delta followed her brother's gaze, but all she saw was Jack Strader in another of his flowered shirts, calmly eating a bowl of banana pudding. She turned back to the sheriff's car, but it was now sitting empty. Where had the officers gone?

"I believe the alleged offender is being brought out at this time, ladies and gentlemen."

The front door of the beauty salon next door to the Geechee Grill opened, and two deputies stepped out onto the sunny sidewalk. Between them, her hands cuffed behind her, stood a scowling woman in curlers and a plastic beautician's cape. The plain woman looked somehow familiar. Delta squinted as she visualized her with makeup, a toothy grin, and perfectly sprayed hair.

"No way! Is that—"

"The sheriff's office is currently in the process of arresting Judith Dempsey, known professionally as Judy Drench, for intentionally vandalizing at least four federally protected turtle nests on Hilton Head. According to a camera operator who worked with Ms. Dempsey, the former newscaster destroyed the nests as a publicity stunt to advance her faltering journalism career. Stay tuned to Channel 1 News for further updates as they become available."

The newsman cleared his throat. "In related news, Judy Drench is no longer affiliated with Channel 1 News."

The officers loaded the handcuffed woman into the back of their car and drove out of the parking lot, blue lights flashing.

"Whoa," Delta said. "She was messing up those nests herself?"

"Of all the nerve!" Tootsie cried, shaking her head.

Jax just laughed. "Think how mad she must be."

"For getting caught?" Delta asked, but Jax shook his head.

"No. For not getting to report the Nest Vandal story anymore!"

28

Coming Back Home

The mid-September sun shone down on the clearing at the heart of Chugeeta Island, where a small group of representatives had gathered for a sacred ceremony. About a dozen members of the Tribal Council were there, as well as the McGee and Wells families. According to Mac, the Tribal Council was requesting that Three Sisters Island be declared a historical preserve so it could never be developed. Even so, this special place looked completely different than it had on the kids' last visit to the islet, right after Hurricane Jackson. The tribe had worked together over the past few weeks to clear much of the fallen timber, preserving three stout trunks that would be carved into totems for the site. Delta hoped one would depict a loggerhead sea turtle.

Without the massive tree in its center, she imagined that an aerial view of the islet would now look like a target—an outer circle of beach, then a ring of dense foliage. Inside that, a halo of open ground surrounded the very core of the little island, the sandy crater that would be the site of today's ceremony.

"I'm glad they didn't rake up all the leaves," she told Darius and Jax. They were standing on a thick carpet of layer upon layer of remnants from the old live oak. Walking on them reminded Delta of being in a bouncy house at a carnival.

Jax nodded. "Yeah, at least *part* of the tree is still here."

"I guess," Darius said. "But whenever my cousins and I would say, 'Let's go to Chugeeta,' we always meant go hang out at the giant tree. That amazing live oak *was* Chugeeta. It just doesn't seem like the same place anymore. It doesn't look familiar."

Delta scanned the sunny clearing. In the center, near the hole left by the triplet trees' destruction, Mac was standing with a friend from the Tribal Council, a chieftess in a traditional Native American costume. They were discussing plans for the sacred rite they were about to perform.

Delta shook her head and smiled. "No, this looks just right."

At Mac's instruction, the assembled group gathered in a semicircle facing the still-gaping crater. The Tribal Council leader raised her hands in the air to reveal that she held three bone carvings in the shape of loggerhead turtles. Mac had said copies of these originals were going to be included in his exhibit at the Santa Elena Discovery Center. The amulets this chieftess held today, though, were the very charms given to the three sisters nearly five hundred years ago. All eyes were on the woman as she began to speak.

"Brothers and sisters, many generations ago our ancestors were blessed with the miracle of triplets born to the cacique of the Orista tribe. The girls' arrival heralded the dawn of a peaceful and prosperous time for our people. Their sign was the sea turtle, which represents a long and fruitful life. So long as the three sisters were together, blessings continued to flow down upon the tribe."

Delta recalled the friendly scene she had witnessed during her first vision in the shell ring. The villagers had been working together happily, laughing and chatting as they completed their daily chores.

"But this good fortune was not to last," the chieftess continued. "One princess was taken from the world at a young age, and the security of the village died with her. These turtle amulets that I now hold are the triplets' own charms, given to them during their lives to represent their bond of sisterhood. Today we place the turtles back into the ground of Three Sisters Island to symbolize their owners' eternal unity."

She carefully placed the turtle carvings into a wooden box held out to her by Mac, who then passed it to another member of the council standing inside the crater. The group watched as this man knelt and delicately positioned the box at the bottom of the hole before clambering back to the surface. Someone then handed the tribal leader a small shovel, which she used to scoop a bit of sandy soil from the edge of the amulets' grave.

"May their souls rest together forever," she said, tossing the shovel's contents into the crater. One by one, everyone present took a turn scooping and tossing dirt onto the wooden box.

After each person had done their part, most of the crowd headed up the path to the beach, where several pontoon boats were waiting to carry them back to Hilton Head. Delta, Jax, and Darius, though, stood staring into the spot where, just a few weeks ago, their favorite tree had been rooted.

"I still think it's sad that the live oak's gone," Darius said, "but I guess its time was just up."

Delta nodded. "Maybe once the three sisters' amulets were together again, the three trees didn't need to be anymore."

"Yeah, and I was thinking," Jax chimed in. "Our bad luck didn't stop the minute I dropped the carving into the hollow trunk, you know. We almost didn't even make it back from Chugeeta. I don't think my turtle was really reunited with the other two until later—when lightning struck and knocked the trees apart. I think *that's* when the curse was really broken."

Delta and Darius considered this theory.

"So y'all think the tree *had* to be destroyed in order to break the curse?"

"It does kind of seem that way," Delta said. "Like it was willing to sacrifice itself to save the tribe."

Mac walked up then to retrieve the shovel someone had left stuck in the ground. "Did I hear y'all talking about the Three Sisters' Curse?"

The kids stared at each other nervously, wondering how much

of their conversation Mac had heard. "Um, we were just saying that, now that the turtle amulets are back together, maybe the tribe won't be cursed anymore."

"Well, Delta, the original tribe dwindled and scattered a long time ago. It doesn't survive as a unit anymore. But even so, maybe better times *are* ahead for the Lowcountry tribes. Hopefully my museum exhibit over in Beaufort will make folks today more aware of the people who lived here before we came along."

Delta smiled and nodded. "In a way, it'll bring the first Carolinians back to life again."

Darius tapped his father on the arm then and pointed into the crater. "Hey, Dad, that hole's not even close to being filled yet."

"Yeah, I know, D. We're going to bring some extra dirt in to finish filling it. Someone mentioned today that there are some saplings growing around the edge of the clearing, probably related to the original tree. The Council was talking about maybe planting one here, on top of the amulets, as a marker. What do y'all think of that idea?"

"That'd be awesome, Mac, but you're only going to plant one young tree?"

"What do you mean, Delta?"

"Well, wouldn't it be nice if you planted three saplings, to replace the triplet trees that fell?"

Mac's face lit up. "That's a great idea! I'll mention it to the Council the next time we meet."

The kids took one last look around the sunny glade that was again the heart of the little island and then followed Mac down the narrow path to the beach. Miss Ruby was already there with Tootsie and Pops, looking out over the water to Hilton Head, with oyster beds and sandbars speckling the space between. Delta noticed that the waving sea grasses on the bars were beginning to turn yellow with autumn's approach, the smell of pluff mud and salt now blended with the scent of drying plants. She watched the tide recede, carrying the glistening waters on out to Port Royal Sound, Santa Elena, and beyond.

"Pops, I was thinking maybe Pedro Menéndez's lost son went to live with a Native American tribe. I mean, I've heard that used to happen sometimes."

"I like to think that's exactly what happened, Delta-boo. I imagine the lost son meeting up with a friendly tribe and living happily to a ripe old age."

Delta, Jax, and Darius looked at each other solemnly and said nothing. They all knew that's not how Juan's story really ended. Laughter wafting toward them across the water broke the somber moment.

"Did you hear that?" Tootsie asked. Both families looked out over the sun-dappled waters of the marsh. "Do you know that sound the tide makes sometimes, pulling against the shore? When it knocks the oyster shells together like it just did, that always reminds me of a young woman giggling."

The adults just laughed, but the three kids smiled knowingly at the dark-haired maiden they—and only they—saw paddling through the maze of swaying grasses.

"What's she still doing here, Darius?" Delta whispered.

"Yeah, we broke the curse," Jax said in a hushed voice, "so shouldn't her spirit be freed now to go on to the great beyond or whatever?"

Darius shook his head. "You know, y'all, I don't think helping people find their way is the Marsh Maiden's *curse*. Since she wasn't able to save Juan Menéndez, I think rescuing other people is her *mission*."

"All aboard!" Mac helped everyone onto the remaining pontoon boat, the pink and lavender sky of the setting sun engulfing them as they slid across the bobbing waves toward home.

"Pops, it's pretty amazing to think all these people have lived here before us and we didn't even know it," Delta said. "Why do you suppose we don't hear more about the native tribes or about the Spanish settlers that were here even before the pilgrims arrived?"

"Delta-boo, I'm afraid that's just the way of the world. History is written by the winners."

"And by those who know how to write," Mac added.

Delta's brow furrowed. "What do you mean?"

"We mean that once the English took ownership of the land that became our country, the Spaniard's story was kind of pushed to the back burner," Pops explained. "And since the Native Americans didn't write their stories down, much of their history was lost."

Surrounded by her brother, grandparents, and friends, Delta thought again of the nearly forgotten princess. Delta didn't even know the girl's name, and no one ever would. The Marsh Maiden was anonymous and alone, but she was still happy to help others whenever she could.

"If nobody's telling those stories, then we should tell them ourselves," Delta said. "That should be *our* mission."

The group was quiet as the boat chugged toward the dock, the Chugeeta clearing behind and the ancient shell ring of Hilton Head just ahead. Farther down the coast lay Port Royal Sound and the ruins of the Santa Elena colony.

Pops put his arm around Delta's shoulders. "So, Delta-boo. Been anytime interesting lately?"

She stifled a laugh. "Oh, Pops. You have no idea!"

Fact or Fiction?

E ven though *The Sea Turtle's Curse* is a fictional novel and Delta and her family are inventions of the author, many of the places, events, and historical figures in the story are based in fact.

🐢 Loggerhead sea turtles lay several hundred nests on the beaches of Hilton Head Island every summer, and each nest holds about a hundred eggs. Sadly, though, less than one in one thousand hatchlings survives to adulthood. You can help improve their chances by leaving marked nests alone, filling any holes left on the beach, and using red covers on flashlights during nesting season.

🐢 The Orista tribe lived year-round on the South Carolina coast for thousands of years, hunting, fishing, and farming. Although the triplets and their mother are fictional characters, the Oristas and other area tribes did have some female chieftains. You can explore the remains of the seven-hundred-year-old Green Shell Ring on Hilton Head, but you *will* have to cut through a graveyard to get to it.

🐢 There are many Native American legends throughout the Southeastern United States, but the story of the Marsh Maiden and the Three Sisters is from the author's imagination. Likewise, while many small islands dot the waters near Port Royal Sound and the real Hilton Head Island, the islet of Chugeeta is fictitious.

🐢 Pedro Menéndez de Avilés did establish the Santa Elena colony in 1566 on what is now Parris Island, and he served from there as governor of the North American continent until his death in 1574. His only son, Juan, really was lost at sea prior to the older Menéndez's arrival, although Juan was believed to have disappeared in the Gulf of Mexico. It is highly unlikely that he would have ended up anywhere near South Carolina.

🐢 Although different in design and layout from the attraction described in *The Sea Turtle's Curse*, there is a real museum devoted to the history of the Santa Elena colony. You can visit the Santa Elena History Center in Beaufort, South Carolina, just upriver from the Parris Island Marine Recruit Depot—the actual archaeological site of the Spanish colony.

🐢 Numerous ships have met their doom in the waters of Port Royal Sound, which is the second-deepest harbor on the Eastern coast of North America. Divers have explored and salvaged goods there from the wrecks of Spanish and French ships dating from the Santa Elena era as well as several sunken Civil War vessels from the 1800s.

🐢 Many meteorites are found in far-northern regions such as Siberia, where Delta's parents were headed, but not because more meteors fall there than in other parts of the world. Scientists believe the dark metallic rocks are simply easier to find in the relatively treeless, snow-covered plains there than in more heavily forested areas.

☛ After learning about the Native Americans and Spanish colonists who once called the Lowcountry of South Carolina home, Delta decides to learn more about her own family's heritage in order to keep her ancestors' stories alive. What is *your* story?

Acknowledgments

Although my name stands alone on the cover, creating this book was the work of many helpful hands and minds. Firstly, great thanks to the folks at Koehler Books for enthusiastically jumping on the Delta and Jax train and making it such an enjoyable ride. For helping me hone the initial manuscript, kudos to my beta readers: Cassandra King Conroy, Patti Callahan Henry, Sheri Levy, Dina Schiff Massachi, Mary Alice Monroe, Terry Roberts Smith, and my fellow scribes at the Island Writers Network. Special appreciation for constant support and encouragement goes to Wayne and Marlene Riley (who always believed I could do it, even when I had my doubts), as well as to Jonathan Haupt, Rockelle Henderson, Sally Sue Lavigne (who happens to own the delightful Storybook Shoppe—the only children's bookstore in the state of South Carolina), Michael Stumm, and my adopted Port Royal Plantation family. Most of all, my eternal love and gratitude go to Steve, Kelly, Brad, Kyla, and Hannah. You make everything worthwhile.

CPSIA information can be obtained
at www.ICGtesting.com
Printed in the USA
JSHW021059081221
21073JS00002B/14